JOSEPH'S BROTHERS SELLING HIM FOR TWENTY PIECES OF SILVER

THE ILLUSTRATED
BIBLE
STORY BOOK
OLD TESTAMENT

Stories retold for children by
SEYMOUR LOVELAND

With an Introduction by
KATHARINE LEE BATES

Illustrated by
MILO WINTER

DOVER PUBLICATIONS, INC.
MINEOLA, NEW YORK

Bibliographical Note

The Illustrated Bible Story Book—Old Testament, first published by Dover Publications, Inc. in 2008, is reproduced from the work first published by Rand McNally & Company, Chicago and New York, in 1923. This edition includes a new audio recording to accompany the text.

International Standard Book Number

ISBN-13: 978-0-486-46844-0
ISBN-10: 0-486-46844-5

Audio recording produced by Blane & DeRosa Productions, Inc.

Manufactured in the United States of America
Dover Publications, Inc., 31 East 2nd Street, Mineola, N.Y. 11501

THE ILLUSTRATED
BIBLE
STORY BOOK
OLD TESTAMENT

THE INTRODUCTION

THESE Old Testament stories, simplified for little hearers and readers, are not meant to take the place of the Bible, but to serve as a foretaste. Even in my own childhood I remember such books. Being the youngest, I had to go to bed first, and while my next older brother was frisking out of his clothes in the room beyond, our mother would read to me from a small blue volume called *Peep of Day*. These stories were of Christ—of His birth in Bethlehem, the riding of the Three Magi on their white camels to bring Him gifts, His boyhood in Nazareth, His love of flowers and birds and lonely places, and of His healing pity, when He grew to be a man, for blindness and weakness and suffering and sin. But I always kept awake to hear the story from my brother's book, thicker, with worn pink binding, *Line upon Line,* which told of the strange life of the desert, where wandering groups of herdsmen pitched their black tents beside the precious wells of water, and shepherds, playing on reed pipes, walked before their flocks of sheep and goats, leading them to green pastures. I grieved for the boy Joseph, the dreamer whom Jacob "loved more than all his children, because he was the son of his old age." What brothers were those to strip the lad of his "coat of many colors" made for him by his father's own withered hands, cast him into a pit, and draw him out only to sell him for twenty pieces of silver to a caravan of gypsy traders that came "from Gilead, with their camels bearing spicery and balm and myrrh" on their far way down to Egypt!

Egypt! I would make pictures for myself of that wonderful valley of the Nile, the river that runs like a ribbon through a long and narrow land, a river bordered by palaces and pyramids and by pillared temples where sat enthroned the giant images of heathen gods, as there, but without offerings and without worshipers, they are sitting still. And Palestine! What child would not love "a land flowing with milk and honey"?

And the things that happened in those enchanting countries, marvels as amazing as any found in my fairy books! A baby floating in a queer bit of a boat among tall green rushes, found by a bathing princess who made him her own son! Bread that fell from heaven every morning! A beaten donkey who rebuked her master! A mighty man whose strength was all in his hair! A witch who could call the dead up from their graves like "gods ascending out of the earth"!

And such heroes! David, the rosy-cheeked boy who slew the giant! Joshua, whose way of making war by marching and shouting and blowing of trumpets was much like mine, only with a more impressive climax! Gideon, who dared break three hundred pitchers at once!

The elder children had their own book, too, *Lines Left Out*, but this they would proudly read to themselves downstairs by the center-table lamp, while I watched them with admiration and secret despair. In those days I thought that I should never master the magic art of reading, for even the alphabet looked like a company of imps, all making faces at one bewildered little girl. Many tears spattered my primer before that hidden wisdom suddenly became my own, but as soon as I could read at all I could read anything. The majestic language of the Bible in the King James Version, made when English speech was at its richest and most poetic, held me even when it did not tell a story. In childhood I heard the whole Bible read aloud again and again, and I never tired of it, for there was always that great tide of music, bearing even Leviticus along.

But this was long ago, in a dreamy Cape Cod village, twenty miles from a railroad, where life was unhurried and there was plenty of time in the morning for family prayers. We all had our favorite seats, our mother and her flock of four, and in these we settled down contentedly after our simple breakfast, each with his own Bible in hand, to read the next chapter in order, whatever it might be. Genealogies with their tongue-twisting names were fun, and for matters that we did not understand we easily substituted some innocent interpretation of our own, like one of the shore boys in school, who loudly and laboriously one morning brought out the verse: "And the sea went down and there was a great clam." For at school, as at home, we read the Bible through, chapter after chapter, book after book, and when we had finished Revelations we turned back to Genesis.

In church, too, we heard long portions of Scripture sonorously intoned from the pulpit, and this part of the service I, for one, always enjoyed. It was almost as pleasant as the hymns and far nicer than "the long prayer," when the bowed figure of my mother, black in her widow's weeds, would often send me into a fit of sobbing, while I flung my small arms about her and tried to tug her erect again. As for sermons, I soon decided that they were not for little people, and by dint of a number of black and white pins, which I kept stuck in the end of the pew cushion, I would beguile sermon time by playing Indian wars and *Uncle Tom's Cabin* on a patient palm-leaf fan. Then followed Sunday school, with recitation of Bible passages learned by heart, and then the delights of a general basket luncheon, and then afternoon church, when tumbled heads nestled drowsily against some beloved shoulder, and then the long walk home—a walk which we children would turn into a game of glorious adventures—and, after supper, hymns and the Westminster catechism till "softly along the road of evening" "Old Nod the shepherd," came.

You see, it was not such a bad thing to be a Puritan child, especially if one's mother had a face and spirit radiant with mirth. And I have come to value as the best of my education that background of Bible lore, that splendor of Bible speech.

To children the Bible is a Wonder Book, appealing to imagination, sympathy and the moral nature. The adult student of Holy Writ realizes that he is dealing with a library of Hebrew history, law, drama, philosophy, poetry — a library whose books were written by various authors and date from different eras; but for childhood the distinction in literature between fable and fact is not important. In the story of Jonah and the Whale, as in the story of St. George and the Dragon, there is spiritual meaning, and it is upon this essential truth that the child's mind naturally fastens. He delights in angels as he delights in fairies, but visions them in the cloudy figures of the sky as he glimpses elves peeping through the wind-swayed grass — beings not to be met on the sidewalk nor made of the same human stuff as aunts and uncles. Perhaps the great heresy, after all, is the heresy of the commonplace. Perhaps the great sin is the refusal of gladness. Thoreau says: "If the day and night are such that you greet them with joy, and life emits a fragrance like flowers and sweet-smelling herbs — is more elastic, starry, immortal — that is your success." It is the success, the very mood, of childhood, that finds this earth a shining chariot, like that wherein Elijah "went up by a whirlwind into heaven."

One of the greatest English writers, John Ruskin, who was born over one hundred years ago, in 1819, the very year in which Queen Victoria was a baby and Abraham Lincoln a barefoot boy of ten, had his young imagination nourished on these stories no less than his sense of the beauty of language developed. He related in manhood how "my mother forced me, by steady daily toil, to learn long chapters of the Bible by heart; as well as to read it every syllable through, hard names and all, from Genesis to the Apocalypse, about once a year."

Among the portions of Scripture which this child of six or seven, his yellow head bent over the page, learned so thoroughly were the whole of the Sermon on the Mount, many psalms and almost the entire book of Revelation. The boy was put at his task soon after his simple breakfast and at it he had to stay till the allotted passage could be recited without a slip. "My mother," he testified later, "never gave me more to learn than she knew I could easily get learnt, if I set myself honestly to work, by twelve o'clock. She never allowed anything to disturb me when my task was set; if it was not said rightly by twelve o'clock, I was kept in till I knew it."

Children are very busy nowadays, all their bright hours are as crowded with engagements as those of their elders. And mothers, always busy, are busier than ever. There are not many mothers now who could give the forenoon to reading with their children, as did Mrs. Ruskin, nor would many of these spend most of the time, as did Mrs. Ruskin, on the Bible. Ruskin has recorded his deep gratitude to this steadfast Scotch mother of his "for the resolutely consistent lessons which so exercised me in the Scriptures as to make every word of them familiar to my ear in habitual music,—yet in that familiarity reverenced, as transcending all thought, and ordaining all conduct."

But even in these breathless times of ours, and with all the variety of children's books and children's interests and children's occupations, there can be found leisure for Bible stories—the stories, for instance, grouped in this volume, stories of Joseph and Moses, Saul and Samuel, David and Jonathan, Solomon and Absalom and the rest. These stories, told for thousands of years by dwellers in the desert, by boatmen on the Nile, by fishermen on the Sea of Galilee, by builders of the Temple at Jerusalem, by Hebrew captives in Nineveh and Babylon, weeping as they remembered Zion, may at first hearing sound to us as voices of the far-away, the long-ago, blown like seeds upon the wind from clime to clime. Yet so richly stored are these tales with passionate life, with the deep wisdom of love and suffering, the bright inspiration of daring, patriotism, friendship, so divine with imagination, mystery, and faith, that they are as young as the youngest heart that hears them.

"Light cometh from the East." Our Bible is the offering of the Orient to Europe and America—an open treasure for all parents who would give good gifts unto their children.

Katharine Lee Bates

THE CONTENTS

JACOB'S WRESTLING AT THE BROOK

BIBLE STORY BOOK

JACOB'S WRESTLING AT THE BROOK

How many of you little people like to go away from home visiting? Perhaps sometimes you have been so far away that you had to ride on the cars. You wanted to sit next to the window, I know, so that you could see all the wonderful things you passed.

Years and years ago, long before your grandfather was a little boy, people liked to travel. They made long visits away from home. But there were no swift cars for people to ride in then. So they walked part of the way and when they grew tired, a camel or donkey would carry them.

This story is about a man who had been away from home on a long, long visit. He really had to make the visit. He had been wicked to his brother. He was afraid his brother would punish him, so he left home and went to live with his uncle and his cousins. He must

often have felt homesick, don't you think so?—especially when he heard that his dear mother had died and left his father alone. I'm sure he wanted to go home and comfort his father. Besides, he began to be ashamed of the way he had treated his brother. And I think he was sorry, too.

When he first came to his uncle's home the man was all alone. But he stayed there for years. He had wives—for in those far-off days a man had more than one wife—and children, and so many servants you couldn't count them, and great flocks of sheep and goats, little lambs and frisky kids, cattle, camels and baby camels, and a pasture full of donkeys. Wouldn't you like to have been there when Jacob—that was the man's name—started back home? When you travel a trunk is all you need. And the baggage car carries that for you.

didn't want to wait a minute, any more than you do when you are going somewhere. So away they marched. Some nights they slept in the wilderness, sometimes on the mountain side. But they did not care where they slept. Their houses were tents which they always carried with them wherever they went. It was easy for them to move, and as easy to sleep wherever they happened to be when night came. Do you think you would like to live that way? It surely would save lots of trouble.

The nearer Jacob came to his home the more afraid he grew of his brother. Esau, his brother, had really forgotten the wicked way Jacob had treated him. But Jacob could not forget. The way he had hurt his brother kept wriggling and twisting in his mind like an ugly snake. Perhaps he was sorry that he had started home.

So he and his whole company halted. He decided he would send some of his servants to his brother Esau with a splendid present. That was Jacob's way of saying he was sorry. And what do you think was Jacob's gift to Esau? Droves of cattle, flocks of sheep and goats; camels and donkeys, so many of them that one man could not manage them. They had to go in separate droves

The only baggage cars Jacob had were his camels and his donkeys. The animals carried baskets or panniers full of food fastened on their sides. Leather bottles of water and great packsaddles were strapped tightly on their backs. All Jacob's flocks and cattle, and his eleven sons with their mothers, must go with him. Do you remember Joseph, the boy who had such strange dreams? He was a small boy when he went on this long journey with his father Jacob. He must have walked beside his mother's camel as they traveled.

All the people were in a great hurry when they started. They

with a driver for each one. Off
the big present started for Esau's tents.
It was growing dark, for night was
coming. Perhaps the moon was shining brightly to show them the way.

It was a splendid place for the
caravan to rest for the night. The
men with the present went on.
Jacob and his company waited by
the river side. It was a small river,
so dry in places that people could
cross over it on foot. But there
was enough water left in spots for
the animals and the thirsty travelers
to have a refreshing drink. Jacob
kept thinking, thinking all the
time, what will Esau do. Would

he be so angry that he would hurt
Jacob's children and their mothers,
perhaps destroy his servants and his
flocks?

Jacob could not rest. He rose
up late in the night when every one
must have been asleep, and called
to his wives and his maidservants:
"Take my eleven sons with you and
cross over the river." The great
company of people and of animals
followed as Jacob went before them
with his family. He did not stay
with them. Back he went to the
other side of the river. He was
alone. He must have thrown himself on the ground with his face
pressed close against it. Jacob

had been wicked and was sorry. He asked God to hear him, and said: "I am not worthy of the least of all the loving-kindnesses.... which thou hast showed unto thy servant."

Then he must have risen from the ground and looked up into the dark blue sky. God had heard. Jacob knew it. Close beside him stood the figure of a man, more of a shadow than a man. He came toward Jacob like a warrior and Jacob fought with him. By the river side the two wrestled until the

darkness of night changed to the light of morning. Jacob was victorious. He had not been thrown down by the other wrestler. But his thigh had been hurt where the man touched him. The hurt made him limp when he walked.

"Let me go," said the man to Jacob. "I cannot stay when the daylight comes."

"Give me a blessing first," answered Jacob, "and tell me your name." But the man, more like a shadow than a man, would not tell Jacob his name.

"What is your name?" he asked Jacob. When Jacob told him his name the man gave him the blessing for which he had asked. And more than that, he gave Jacob a wonderful new name. Jacob was to be called Israel, which means seeing God. He had "prevailed" with God and with men. He had won with God, for he was sorry he had done wrong. He would win with his brother, for he was going to be kind to him.

When the sun rose high and hot in the sky Jacob crossed over the river again. He was happy now. Esau saw him and ran and kissed him. He had forgotten all about that bad time so long ago. Perhaps Jacob forgot it too. God had blest him.

STORIES OF JOSEPH AND HIS BROTHERS

JOSEPH THE DREAMER

How many of you children have ever played house in a tent? Do you know that a long time ago nearly everybody lived in tents? In those days the people moved so often it seemed foolish to build houses. Tents could be folded up easily and strapped on a camel's or donkey's back. The people always pitched their tents close to a sparkling stream of water in the middle of fields where there grew plenty of long green grass. Their sheep and cattle were always a hungry lot. It was never long before the animals had nibbled away all of the grass and left the ground brown and bare. Sometimes the sun was so hot that the wells and springs of water dried up. When all the grass and water had disappeared then the people knew it was time to move.

And away they went. Long lines of camels went first. Boys with heavy sticks followed, driving the camels and donkeys. Old people hobbled along trying to keep up with the shouting men and boys. Sleepy babies on donkeys' backs were bounced about as they hurried along.

Mothers kept calling to their children not to lag behind. And a happy, dancing lot of little folks kicked up the dust with their bare heels as they hurried after their mothers. On and on they went. They never stopped until they found fresh fields of grass and wells filled with water.

One of the men who lived in a tent in those long-ago days was very rich and very old. The name of this man was Jacob and, you remember, he had a large family — twelve sons as well as a daughter. Just think of it! A family as big as that would never be lonesome. The ten older sons were kept busy feeding their father's sheep and cattle. They worked in the fields, too. Jacob had wheat fields and his sons

cut the ripe grain and bound it into bundles.

Jacob loved one of his boys better than he did any of the other children. He loved his son Joseph so dearly that he gave the boy a wonderful coat. It must have been soft and lustrous. It was so long that it came down to his heels. And most wonderful of all, the sleeves were so long they almost covered his hands. Not one of Joseph's brothers had a coat like this. When they slept out in the fields his ten elder brothers had nothing to wear but coarse, hairy goat skins. When they were at home in their tents they had nothing to put on but long, loose cotton shirts which they slipped on over their heads. It made all of them very angry to see their younger brother Joseph walking about in his handsome coat.

There were other reasons why the brothers .hated Joseph. The older boys sometimes did very wicked and cruel things. Joseph was always good and kind. Now no one who is bad likes any one else to be good. Then, Joseph had such very queer dreams. Once he dreamed that he and his brothers were in the fields binding the wheat into big bundles. These bundles were called sheaves. Then in his dream a very strange thing happened. Joseph's sheaf stood up straight and tall. But his brothers' sheaves did not stand up. Their sheaves all came and lay down flat on the ground before Joseph's sheaf. When Joseph told his brothers this dream they were very angry and hated him more than ever. "Does this boy think we are going to bow down to him and obey him?" they asked one another.

In another dream Joseph thought the sun and the moon and eleven of the stars left the blue sky and came to where he lay asleep. And the sun and moon and the eleven stars kept bowing and bowing to him as though he was a great man. Joseph said the sun and the moon in his dream were like his father and mother, and that the eleven twinkling stars all had faces like his brothers. Jacob, his father, and the brothers wondered how a poor shepherd boy like Joseph would ever become a great man. "Shall Joseph be like a king some day and rule over us?" the brothers asked one another. "Not if we can help it," they all answered.

But the wicked brothers were mistaken. Joseph's dream did come true. And what do you think? It was his brothers who helped it to come true.

JOSEPH SOLD INTO EGYPT

I told you in the last story that the people who lived in the country where Joseph did had to move very often. Suppose every time you wanted a drink of water you had to move into a new house. People would never know where to find you, would they? Joseph's ten older brothers traveled a great deal. Their sheep and cattle drank so much water it kept the brothers all busy hunting for fresh watering places. One morning Joseph started out to find his brothers. They had been away from home for a long time, so long that their father Jacob wanted to hear from them. He wished to know if they were well, and if the boys and their flocks were getting enough to eat. There

were no letter-boxes nor postmen in those days. If you wanted to know anything about anybody you had to go and find out for yourself.

Jacob wanted to know what his ten older sons were doing, so he sent Joseph to them to find out. Joseph did a very foolish thing before he started. He put on his beautiful long coat with sleeves. He could not walk very fast with his coat flapping about his feet. By the time he reached Shechem, where he expected to find his brothers, they had moved away. He knew, though, where to go. He must follow the empty wells until he came to wells that were full of water. A well full of water always had plenty of grass around it. Joseph knew he would find his brothers and their flocks near grass and water.

The brothers saw Joseph coming. "Let us kill him," they said. "We will say a wild beast has killed him." Only angry, hateful thoughts were in their hearts. They did not care even for the poor father who would grieve so if Joseph were lost. Reuben, the eldest brother, would not have him killed. Reuben was kinder than the other boys. He wanted to save Joseph and take him back to his father. But there was only one Reuben and there were nine rough, ugly brothers. These nine wicked men seized Joseph as soon as he came to their tents. They tore his beautiful coat from him and threw him into an empty cistern. "It is so deep he cannot get out," his brothers said. "Let him stay there until he starves to death."

Some people are dreadfully cross when they are hungry, but after they have had their dinner they feel much more kindly. Joseph's brothers were that way. After they threw Joseph into the cistern they sat down and ate their dinner. When they were through their dinner they did not care so much about killing Joseph. "Let us sell him instead," said his brother Judah. All the brothers thought this was much better. If he were sold he couldn't bother them any more by walking around in his grand coat and telling his dreams.

Very soon a long caravan stopped at their well. This caravan was a long line of camels, donkeys, men, and women on their way to a country called Egypt. "Joseph shall be sold for a slave and taken to Egypt," said the brothers. Then they ran to the empty cistern and drew out the boy. While they were binding his feet so tightly that the cords cut into his flesh, a man in the caravan was counting out twenty shiny silver pieces. These silver pieces he gave to the brothers, who put them into the little bags they always carried inside their belts. Then the man who bought Joseph threw him across the back of a camel and carried him away to Egypt.

Do you suppose the brothers let Joseph take his beautiful coat away with him? No, indeed! They killed a little goat and put its blood into a rough stone basin. Then they dipped the lovely coat with its long sleeves into the basin until it was all stained with blood. In a few days the cruel brothers went home to their father Jacob. They took the beautiful lustrous coat of Joseph and carried it, all torn and bloody, to their father Jacob. They asked him if this coat belonged to Joseph.

They did not tell their father that they had torn the coat off Joseph. No, indeed, they told a lie about it. They said that they had found the coat all torn and bloody in the field. Of course the poor father knew the coat as soon as he looked at it. He said: "It is my son's coat; an evil beast hath devoured him. Joseph is without doubt torn in pieces."

Then Jacob tore his own coat and put ashes on his head. He was so sad that great tears rolled down his cheeks. He said he would feel sorrowful all his life and that he would mourn for Joseph every day. And those hard-hearted brothers let their father mourn over the young lad and believe he was dead. And all this time Joseph was alive and on his way to Egypt.

THE BUTLER'S DREAM

While Jacob was crying in his tent for his lost boy, Joseph was riding along toward Egypt on a camel's back. He was hungry and thirsty, for his brothers had given him nothing to eat or to drink. How the sun did scorch his back during the day! The wind tossed tiny grains of sand into his eyes and made them smart. Poor boy, nobody seemed to care for him, no one was kind to him.

But Joseph did not fret. He knew the kind, cool night was coming, and the friendly stars with their bright fingers would point the way to a well of water. And they

did. The caravan stopped beside the well and rested for the night. What do you all suppose Joseph thought about as he lay down beside his camel? Perhaps he thought of his dream when the star faces had looked so like his brothers.

As soon as the caravan reached Egypt Joseph was sold to Potiphar, one of the king's officers. Joseph was a handsome boy. He never looked cross nor sulky. His master did not put him to work in the fields but gave him something to do in the house. "I like a cheerful face in the house," Potiphar must have said. Joseph seemed to know

22

the very best way to do everything. His master noticed that everything did well with Joseph, so Potiphar made him ruler over his household and over his fields. If Joseph felt homesick he never told any one about it. He knew that great people never whined, and he was going to be great. Almost all boys and girls are sure they will do great things when they grow up.

A very unhappy thing happened. A wicked person began to tell false stories about Joseph. When Potiphar heard these stories he grew angry with Joseph and shut him up in prison. To be stolen from his home and taken to a strange country was bad enough, but think how terrible it must have been to live in a dark, damp prison, perhaps in a cellar full of rats and mice. Joseph loved everything. That was the reason he never was afraid. So if he was thrown into a room with rats and mice he must have loved the little creatures. Instead of hurting them I'm sure he tamed them and perhaps taught them funny tricks.

The jailor watched Joseph and saw that the prisoners were happier and worked more willingly when Joseph was near. "God must be with this boy, and if God is with him he can manage the prison better than I can," thought this sensible jailor. So Joseph was made ruler over the prison and the prisoners. He did not have any more strange dreams but he was able to tell other people what their dreams meant.

In the same prison with Joseph was the king's butler. One night he had a strange dream. It worried him. He decided he would ask Joseph in the morning what it all meant. He was careful to remember it so that he might be able to tell Joseph every bit of it. The butler dreamed that he was out of doors looking at a vine which had three branches. Soon tiny green shoots appeared on the bare branches, then blossoms, and at last heavy clusters of purple grapes hung on the vine. But that was not all. He dreamed

that he held Pharaoh's cup in his hand and began to squeeze the juice of the grapes into the cup. As soon as the cup was full he gave it to Pharaoh, the king.

"Your dream means," said Joseph, "that in three days you will leave the prison and again be Pharaoh's butler." And it all happened just as Joseph had told him. But one thing did not happen that ought to have happened. The butler should have remembered Joseph and told the king about him. But instead of remembering he forgot his kind friend as soon as he reached Pharaoh's palace. A long, long time afterward, however, the butler did remember Joseph, and why he remembered our next story will tell us.

THE FAT AND LEAN COWS

Every day after the butler left the prison Joseph must have gone to the window to watch for him. You know how you watch when you are expecting some one. Joseph was sure the butler would remember him. He might have to wait a long time but he was going to keep watching until some one came for him. For two years Joseph waited. Then one day he saw some men running toward the prison. They seemed to be in a great hurry. As soon as the men reached the prison they called for Joseph and told him that Pharaoh the king wanted to see him. "Don't keep Pharaoh waiting," they said.

Joseph was in a hurry to leave the prison but when he went to the palace he wished to be clean. He knew that every one likes clean boys better than dirty ones, so he stopped to wash and put on fresh clothes.

Pharaoh had had a queer dream. He was worried about it. No one in all his country could tell him what it meant. Then the chief butler remembered Joseph. He went straight to Pharaoh and told him about the wonderful man in prison who could tell people what their dreams meant. If Joseph understood dreams, Pharaoh decided he must

24

JOSEPH TELLING PHARAOH THE MEANING OF HIS DREAM

see him at once. So he sent for him.

You and I do not worry about our dreams. We don't think they are even worth remembering. If you or I had dreamed that we stood by the river and saw seven fine, fat cows come out of the water, we would not have thought anything about it. But if seven lean, sickly cows followed them and ate up the fat ones, and were still leaner, we surely would have been astonished. Cows do not eat meat, they eat grass. So when Pharaoh in his dream saw seven hungry-looking cows eating seven fat cows he was sure it meant something. And it did.

Joseph told him the seven fat cows meant that Egypt was to have seven prosperous years. Prosperous means having all you want of everything. After the seven years of plenty there would come seven years of famine. Those seven miserable starved-looking cows the king saw in his dream meant that a dreadful famine was coming to Egypt.

There isn't a little child here who knows what a famine is, because every one of you gets enough to eat. Suppose sometime when you were hungry there was nothing in your house to eat. If you went to the grocery, the market, or the bakery and asked for something to eat the clerks would shake their heads and tell you there was no food in any of the shops. Perhaps they would let you peek into the empty drawers or try to find something on the bare shelves. You could find no food anywhere. The clouds were keeping all the rain to themselves instead of giving the thirsty earth a drink. Every green thing that grows out of the ground had died because it could not have a drink. When things are that way there is a famine in the country.

For seven years the people of Egypt were to be hungry. But Joseph told them what to do. While they had plenty to eat the people should save their food instead of wasting it. When the wheat grew tall every summer the farmers should cut it down. "But don't grind it all up into flour," Joseph said. He told them to build large storehouses and fill them full of wheat. Every kind of food that could be packed away was to be put in the storehouses. When the long famine time came Egypt would have something to eat. The people of other countries would be hungry because they had not stored away any food.

Do you think Joseph went back to prison after he told Pharaoh what his dream meant? No, indeed! Pharaoh gave Joseph some clothes just like his own. He put a gold chain around his neck, and took the ring from his own finger and put it on Joseph's. Pharaoh thought that a man as wise as Joseph should rule over all the country; so he made him ruler over Egypt. Joseph was now a great man. He lived in a big house, wore fine clothes, and rode in a handsome chariot next after the king. Everybody obeyed Joseph.

When the hungry time came, the people from other countries went to Egypt to buy food. An old, old man in another country grew very hungry. He had eleven sons who were hungry, too. Their cattle and their sheep were dying. There was no grass or hay for them to eat. What should they do? The old man was Joseph's father, Jacob. He heard there was a great man in Egypt who was selling food to hungry people. He did not know that this great man was his lost son Joseph. He and his sons and their families must have food right away or they would all die. So Jacob sent ten of his sons down to Egypt to buy wheat and food. These ten sons were Joseph's wicked brothers who had sold him into Egypt. But the brothers had forgotten all about Joseph. All they thought about was buying food to keep themselves and their little children from starving.

Off the brothers went to Egypt with their donkeys and their empty sacks, and soon came to Joseph's palace. As soon as the ten men saw Joseph they jumped down from their donkeys and lay flat on the ground before him. Here were all Joseph's hungry brothers kneeling before him and asking him to sell them something to eat. He knew his brothers but they did not know him. He remembered the time when he was a boy and lay asleep in the fields with his brothers. He remembered the queer dream he had had, that dream in which all his brothers' sheaves of wheat came and lay down flat on the ground before his sheaf. So Joseph's dream came true.

JOSEPH FORGIVES HIS BROTHERS

Do you think Joseph was glad to see his brothers? No, not at first. But he did want to hear about his father, Jacob, and his youngest brother, Benjamin. So he asked the brothers about their homes, their father, and Benjamin. He did not see Benjamin with them. Perhaps he thought these rough men had got rid of Benjamin as they had of him. So he spoke roughly to them and called them spies. When he learned that his father was alive and that Benjamin was at home with his father, Joseph was kinder to the ten brothers who were kneeling before him.

Jacob was a rich man. He and his sons had plenty of money, but people can't eat money, no matter how hungry they are. And if there is nothing to buy, money isn't worth much, is it? Egypt had plenty of wheat and grain. Canaan, where Jacob lived, had none. The ten brothers had come to Egypt with their pockets full of money. It was only in Egypt that there was any food to buy.

The donkeys that had carried the brothers into Egypt did not carry them all back again. Nine brothers walked back to Canaan, I am sure. Joseph had crammed their empty sacks so full of grain and food that the donkeys would not have strength to carry more than those heavy sacks. And what do you think the brothers found in their sacks when they reached home? When those bulging sacks were opened every man found his money in his sack. Joseph had made them a present of the wheat. At first the brothers were frightened, but they needed food and so they kept the wheat.

But such a big family as Jacob's soon ate all the wheat that was in the sacks. All of them were hungry again. Back to Egypt the brothers must go for more wheat. But at first they would not go because Jacob did not want to let Benjamin go with them. "We will all have to stay here and starve," said one of the brothers. "The lord of Egypt who sells the wheat told us he would not see us again

unless Benjamin came with us." There was nothing to do but let Benjamin go back to Egypt with his brothers. With him Jacob sent a present of nuts, spices, and honey to the great man in Egypt. Jacob thought a present would soften the great man's heart. And all this time he never knew the great man was his own son Joseph.

As soon as the brothers reached Egypt they hurried to Joseph's palace. Their little children were starving at home and they must get back with the wheat as fast as they could travel. Joseph was glad to see them because Benjamin, the brother he loved best, was with them. He made a great feast for

them. He gave them all plenty to eat, but he put more on Benjamin's plate than he did on the plate of any of the others.

Joseph wanted to see his father again and he wanted to keep Benjamin with him. He asked every Egyptian to leave the room so that he could be alone with his brothers. Just imagine how astonished those rough men were when Joseph said, "I am Joseph, your brother whom ye sold into Egypt." Were they glad to hear it? Not at first, for I think they were a little bit frightened. What would Joseph do to them? Can you guess? He kissed them all and forgave them. He told them the terrible famine would last five years longer. "Bring my father to Egypt," he said. "Bring your

little children, your sheep, and your cattle. Don't leave a single thing that belongs to you. Come here and live near me."

Donkeys are not very comfortable to ride on. The babies and their mothers would get very tired riding on them all the way from Canaan to Egypt. So Pharaoh, the king, told Joseph to send plenty of wagons back with the brothers. "Your old father, Jacob, and the little children with their mothers, will be more comfortable riding in wagons," said Pharaoh.

What a bustle and stir there must have been when the brothers reached home again with the wonderful news that Joseph was alive and had invited them all to come to Egypt and live near him! In those days it was not very much work to move. I think it must have been great fun. They just pulled up their tents and folded them and then strapped them on a camel's or a donkey's back. Big boys and little boys drove the sheep and cattle. The animals were glad to go. They knew that moving meant they were going toward wells of water and a place where they could get more to eat. Moving day was a happy day for every one. So off they started, Jacob and his big family, and went down into Egypt to live near Joseph.

STORIES OF MOSES AND JOSHUA

THE FINDING OF MOSES

When your mother has company how does she want you to behave? She wants you to be polite and treat the guests kindly, does n't she? When we have company we do all sorts of nice things to make them happy. Would you like to hear a story about a king who invited company to his country? He was the king of Egypt. His guests were the Hebrew people. The king told the Hebrews to bring everything they owned with them— their camels, donkeys, oxen, sheep, tents, and of course their wives and all their children. "You need never go home again," the king told them. "There is plenty of room in my country, Egypt, for all of you, and I want you to stay with me."

So the Hebrews stayed. But when the king died his wicked grandson wanted the country all for himself. He forgot that the Hebrew people had been invited to come to Egypt and were really company. He was very cruel to them. He treated them like slaves instead of guests. The Hebrews worked very hard making bricks and building

baby boy. She knew God would help her if she prayed to Him. So she asked God to help her save her baby.

If you had gone into her mud hut one day you would have seen her squatting on the floor weaving a basket. She was making it out of coarse, strong rushes that grew on the river bank. You would not have known that a baby was in the house, everything was so still and quiet. But a baby was there, hidden away where no one could find him.

What do you suppose the Hebrew mother was going to do with the basket when it was finished? She was going to put the baby boy in it and hide it among the tall reeds in the river. She covered the basket inside and out with a sticky pitch and slime. No water could get into a basket that had been covered with this gummy stuff. The dear little fellow would be safe in his floating basket.

The baby had an older sister named Miriam. She helped her mother find a nice, safe place in the river among the tall, thick rushes where they could put the baby in his water cradle. There they carried the baby one morning. He was fast asleep. It was so early that he had not yet waked for his

storehouses for the king, who did not give them any time to rest. "Hard work will kill them," thought the king. But God was with the Hebrews and He made them so strong that the hard work did not hurt them.

"What shall we do with these Hebrews?" the king asked his soldiers. "They will soon be stronger than we and then they will own our country." So he did a terrible thing. He ordered all the Hebrew boy babies to be drowned in the river.

There was one Hebrew mother who did not intend to drown her

THE PRINCESS FINDS MOSES IN THE RIVER

breakfast. Tiny babies are almost always asleep when they are not hungry.

His mother went back to her hut. But Miriam sat on the river bank and watched her little brother in his boat.

Soon something happened. The beautiful princess, daughter of the wicked king, came down to the river for her morning bath. "What a very strange place for such a pretty basket!" she must have said when she saw the baby's boat swaying in the river among the rushes. She told her maids to get the basket and bring it to her. Just imagine her surprise when she opened the basket and found the pretty baby in it! He was awake now and hungry and he began to cry.

The princess must have kissed him and cuddled him in her arms, for she loved little babies. "You are a Hebrew baby, but I am going to keep you for my own. You shall be my little boy," the princess said.

Miriam was very happy to see the beautiful princess cuddling her tiny brother. "Shall I get you a nurse for him?" Miriam asked her. The princess told her to go and find a woman who would care for the baby. Can you guess where Miriam

went and whom she brought back with her to the riverside? Straight home to her mother she ran as fast as her feet could carry her. It was his own mother that was to nurse and care for the tiny baby until he was old enough to go to the king's palace and live with the princess as her son.

Can you guess the Hebrew baby's name? Remember, he was a water baby, for the princess found him in the water. And because she drew him out she named him Moses, which in our language means drawn out.

EGYPT AND THE RED SEA

You remember that the Egyptians invited the Hebrews to come and live in their country. In time they grew tired of their guests. Jacob and Joseph and the king who had been kind to them died. The new king and his people treated the Hebrews very cruelly. But they did not want the Hebrews to leave Egypt. Why not? The Hebrews worked hard and built big storehouses and cities for the Egyptians.

"Let us make slaves of these people," the Egyptians said. Now that kind Pharaoh and Jacob and Joseph had gone, the Egyptians probably thought the Hebrews had no friends. But they were mistaken. The Hebrews had the greatest friend in all the world. That friend was God. Besides, there was a Hebrew named Moses who was always listening for God's voice. And when a man or a little boy or a little girl is listening for God to speak in his or her heart, He always does. So God spoke to Moses and told him to take his people out of Egypt and into a big, beautiful country He would give them to be their own.

The people were afraid at first. They would have to cross a wilderness before they could reach the country God meant to give them. But Moses knew the way and he was not afraid. The Hebrews did not start at once. There was a great deal to be done before they could be ready. Some days Pharaoh, the king, told them they might leave the country, and just as they were ready to start he would send them a message and tell them to stay where they were.

Finally God spoke to Moses and told him it was time for them to go. There was no use waiting any longer. Moses told the people to be ready. "Dress for traveling, draw up your long coats and bind them around your waists, have on your walking shoes, and every one of you carry a staff." They were to eat their supper before they started. They stood up while they ate. They were in too big a hurry to sit down. Not a crumb of bread nor a morsel of meat were they to leave behind them. Even their bread boards were strapped together with their clothes upon their backs. The bread not ready to be baked they must carry with them. Just as soon as the signal came they must start. Not a minute could be wasted.

What do you suppose that signal was? Moses had told the people and told Pharaoh that at midnight

country. And then midnight came. In every Egyptian house there was crying and mourning. Fathers and mothers were sobbing bitterly and little children were calling for their parents.

"Up, it is time to go!" Moses called. And the Hebrews went. The Egyptians followed after them, urging the Hebrews to hurry out of their country as fast as they could. "Take away everything that belongs to you, don't leave a thing behind," the Egyptians said to the marching Hebrews.

Shut your eyes and try to see that long line of cattle, camels, sheep, goats, little folks, big folks, and babies on their way through the town, marching across the meadows and on toward the sea. The moon sailing through the sky looked down on them just as it will look down on you the next time it peeks through your window. What wonderful stories that moon could tell us if only it could speak!

No sooner were the Hebrews out of sight and out of his country than Pharaoh began to wish that he had not allowed them to go. "Who will do our hard work for us now?" the Egyptians asked. "Come, let us go after them." Chariots were brought. Horses were harnessed. Some men must have ridden on dromedaries,

something dreadful was going to happen in Egypt. And when that dreadful thing came the Hebrews were to leave the country at once. In every house at midnight some one would die. "Sprinkle the blood of a lamb on your doors," Moses told the Hebrews. "These red stains will show that you are God's people, and that no one in your houses will die."

How could those red stains be seen in the dark? That night it was not dark. The moon was big and full. In Egypt when the moon shines it is very light, much lighter than when the moon shines in our those swift camels that are said to move as fast as the wind. What a scrambling there must have been as the Egyptians ran after the Hebrews!

Where were the Hebrews all this time? They were resting quietly on the shores of the Red Sea. They were out of Egypt and felt very thankful—for a little while. But they were great people to fret and complain if anything went wrong. A Hebrew looked up and saw the Egyptians coming. Do you suppose he said, "God has saved us once from the Egyptians, and he will do it now?" No, indeed! His knees probably knocked together and his teeth chattered as he and all the rest of the Hebrews said to Moses: "Why did you bring us out of Egypt? It was better for us to work hard and live there than for us to die here in this wilderness."

What did Moses answer? No doubt something like this: "Keep quiet, don't be afraid. See what God will do for you." Then Moses stretched his hand out over the sea. God had told him to "go forward." He would make a path for the people through the sea. The Egyptians were behind them, the deep sea in front of them. As Moses held his hand over the sea a fierce wind began to blow. The

waves of the sea rippled along the shore. Then they foamed and roared as you have seen the lakes and ocean do when the wind is strong. The waters piled up on each side, and there, just ahead of them, was a strip of sand right through the sea. A path had been made for them by the hand of God. High walls of water were on each side of the people as they crossed safely over to the other side of the sea.

After them came the Egyptians. They plunged into the sea and tried to cross on that narrow strip of

BREAD FROM HEAVEN

After the Hebrews had passed through the Red Sea they were in the wilderness. Not a house nor a tent was to be seen anywhere. Some large birds probably followed them out of Egypt and flapped their wings high over their heads. Some little folks may have been afraid of them and said, "See, they are chasing us." And that is exactly what the birds were doing. Those great birds always followed a caravan or an army.

On the Hebrews marched. They had a long way to go and they must walk quickly. Soon the Red Sea was far behind them. The ground was rough and stony. Bleak mountains began to rise all around them. "What kind of country is this?" the Hebrew people asked Moses. "You told us you would take us into a beautiful land where we could have plenty of milk to drink and honey to eat."

"We must cross the desert first," Moses told them. "The lovely country we are marching toward is beyond those mountains."

The people could not march all the time. Even the animals grew tired and wanted to lie down and rest. When night came the long caravan of people, animals, with little

sand. What a terrible time they were having! Their chariot wheels came off and they probably tumbled over each other. The wind stopped blowing and back the waters rolled over the strip of sand. The terrified Egyptians could not get out when the waters rolled back. They were drowned — horses, men in chariots, and the king's soldiers.

The Hebrews were safe on the opposite shore. The Egyptian king could not be cruel to them any more. And they were singing a song of thanksgiving to God, who had saved them from Egypt and the sea.

children, some walking, some riding, came to a halt. The fathers set up the tents. Big brothers milked the goats so that the little children could have their supper. Mothers and big sisters baked the dough they had brought with them out of Egypt. How comfortable it must have been to lie on the warm goatskin beds! No cruel master would whip them out of those beds in the morning, for Egypt was far behind them. I hope before they went to sleep that night they said "thank you" in their hearts for all the kindness God was showing them.

Every day they marched farther and farther into the desert. The big boys and the men must have been kept busy watching the flocks of goats and sheep. There were

fierce lions and leopards prowling about. These hungry animals were just waiting to pounce on some little lamb or kid and carry it away.

At last all the food the Hebrews had brought with them out of Egypt had been eaten. Not a crumb was left of the bread the people had baked in the wilderness. What should they do? Starve? The people thought so, and then they began to fret and complain again.

"Why did we leave Egypt and all those good things we had to eat there?" the Hebrews asked each other. They went to Moses and spoke to him angrily. They told

had none. "In the morning you shall have bread," Moses told the people, "plenty of it, enough for all of you."

All the little hungry girls and boys went to sleep that night wondering how God could send them bread from heaven. God had told Moses that He would rain bread from heaven for them to eat. Perhaps each little child listened in the darkness to hear the thumpity thump of bread cakes falling on tent roofs. But no such sound did they hear. Now and then a wolf would howl or a jackal would scream. Those were the only noises except the dogs barking as they watched the sheep.

Morning came. We can see the little folks jump from their beds

him that he had brought them into this wilderness to starve them to death. Were they not wicked to say such unkind things to the friend who was trying so hard to help them?

But God was with Moses and showed him what to do for the angry people. The Hebrews had plenty of sheep, goats, and cattle with them. If they have been as hungry as they said they were they could have eaten some of their own animals. But the people wanted bread. Babies couldn't eat meat. They could eat bread, and they

and peek out of the tent doors to see if the bread had come. How many disappointed little faces there must have been! There was not a morsel of bread anywhere, only heavy drops of dew upon everything.

The sun came out and drank up all the dew. And then, all over the ground, on shrubs and bushes where the dew had been, were small round things which had not melted. They hung on leaves and twigs and branches. They were round and white like the children's own little cakes of bread.

"What is it?" the people asked Moses. "It is the bread which Jehovah hath given you to eat," he answered them. He told them to gather all they needed just for that one day. Every morning this bread would come with the dew. "You shall have it fresh every morning," Moses told them.

It wasn't made of dough but it was *so* good to eat. It tasted sweet as honey. And it was rich, too, as though oil had been put into it when it was made. You know how much better things that are made with butter taste than if they are made with some other fat or with oil. We all like cake which is made with butter. Where the Hebrews lived they often made things with oil instead of butter.

"What is it?" the people kept asking. They wanted a name for it. And what do you think they called it? Manna—the very best kind of name for it, for manna means "What is it?"

God had fed them. Not one went hungry. Every morning for forty years this manna came with the dew. Every day that the people were in the wilderness God showed that He cared for them. They never knew what this "manna" was. It was food. That was enough. It came from God. By this the people knew God loved them and would never leave them.

THE FACE OF MOSES

Did you ever try to listen to some one read a story when the phonograph was going, the baby crying, and when other people in the room were talking and laughing? Perhaps you said to the one who was reading to you, "Let us go into the next room where it is quiet. I can hear better there."

That was why Moses went up into the mountain to talk with God. He wanted to get away from the noisy, shouting people. He could not listen to their din and hear God at the same time. Moses knew Jehovah, God, wanted to help his people if they were willing to be helped. Of course, he could do nothing for them if they would not let him. The people Moses was trying to teach were hard to please. Sometimes they forgot Moses and forgot God and did the very things that would hurt them.

When Moses came down from the mountain he heard the people singing and saw them dancing around the image of a great golden calf. He did not feel sorry because they were playing. He was glad to have them happy. But the people were calling the silly golden idol, God. More than that, they were saying that this image had saved them from Egypt and had given them food.

This was not true, and it made Moses angry. It made him so angry that he threw down the two tablets of stone he was carrying and broke them in pieces. On these stones were written ten commandments. Moses had brought them down from the mountain to read to his people. And here they were worshiping a golden idol and not wishing to hear a word about God or His commandments! I'm not surprised that Moses was discouraged and broke the stones.

He did more than break the stone tablets. He destroyed the golden calf—ground it into powder, and

GOD TALKED WITH MOSES ON THE MOUNTAIN TOP

threw it into a brook. After that he went back on the mountain top. He carried some fresh stones with him, for the commandments must be written over again. Perhaps he was wondering how God could make those wicked, idolatrous people over into good people. When he was on the mountain top God gave Moses a message which told him how he could do it. He could help them by loving them.

When Moses went up the mountain the stones he carried must have felt very heavy. Perhaps he thought that all those wonderful commandments would not be given to him again. When one has a heavy heart everything else seems heavy. He may have been wondering what those foolish people would do when he was away from them this time. Of one thing Moses was certain, they could not make another golden calf, for he had taken away all their gold.

Up, up, he went, so high that he left even the clouds behind him. You know that the tops of tall mountains always reach above the clouds. It was on the top of the mountain that God talked with Moses. God was not angry with the people, only very sorry for them because they were so foolish as to think that a golden idol could help them.

Then God gave Moses a very comforting message. It was this: "Jehovah is a God merciful and gracious, slow to anger, and abundant in loving-kindness and truth; keeping loving-kindness for thousands, forgiving. . . . sin."

Moses was on the mountain forty long days and nights. He had nothing to eat or to drink, but he was neither tired nor hungry. All that God had told him before he told him again, and the ten commandments were written upon the stone tablets. When Moses was ready to come down again to his people his face beamed with joy. I think he came down more quickly than he went up,

for he was much happier. I have seen very little folks drag their feet after them as though those feet were made of lead. And I knew why. Those little folks were unhappy. But how those small heels do caper along the walk when their owners are happy!

When Moses came back his people were watching for him, but they ran away as soon as they saw him. He frightened them, not because he did or said anything to them but because his face shone with a wonderful light. They were willing to have him read the commandments to them, and they wanted to hear what God had told him. Of course, Moses did not want to turn his back to them while he was reading. When we are talking to people we like to turn our faces toward them because they can hear us better. But Moses' face was so bright and shone so with happiness that the people could not bear to look at it. So he wore a veil over his face in order that the light which shone in his face should not blind the people as he read.

Moses talked with God a great many times afterward, but he never wore the veil when he did so. It was only when Moses talked with his people that he had to wear a veil.

THE TALKING DONKEY

Balaam was a very wise man. The people of the country in which he lived thought he knew everything and could help them out of all sorts of trouble. The Moabites were his neighbors and they were in dreadful trouble. They had refused to let the Hebrews or Israelites pass through their country although the Hebrews had promised not to take a thing nor to hurt a single person.

But the Moabites didn't want to be friendly. They wanted to fight. Now when they saw the tents of Israel pitched by the riverside they were badly frightened. Such a great company of people! So many of them that Balak, king of Moab, was sure the Hebrews would defeat him in battle.

The Hebrews were no longer afraid. They obeyed their leader Joshua instead of finding fault with him.

The land God had promised Israel was just across the river from their camp. Joshua had told them it was time to march into it. And they marched. Of course they were willing to go in peaceably and possess the land. But if Moab insisted on fighting, the Hebrews were ready to fight. They did not want to

"You must curse Israel for us," they replied. "Balak says there are so many of these Hebrews that they will eat up our country as an ox eats grass."

Balaam knew that he could not curse Israel, for God had blessed those people. He was wise enough to know that he could not interfere with God. Cursing, you know, is wishing evil things for people — being glad that they are having trouble. When God sends good to his people nobody can prevent its coming to them. But Balaam wanted those handsome presents and all that money Balak had sent to him if he would only come and curse Israel. Balaam thought only of the many fine things he could buy with a bag full of money.

So, wise as he was, he acted foolishly and started out with the king's messengers to do the very thing he knew he could not do. He called two of his servants to go with him, saddled his ass, and trotted down the road toward Moab. It must have been a bright, beautiful day. The sun was shining and the wind playing with the leaves of the trees. Great purple grapes just ready to be eaten hung over the vineyard walls. It was early morning and all of the people felt rested after a long night's sleep. Every

run away from danger any more nor did they wish they were back in Egypt as they did that time by the Red Sea.

What was Balak to do since he had gotten himself into all this trouble? Ask Balaam about it, of course. Surely the wise man could help him. Off posted two Moabites to Balaam's tent and found him sitting in its doorway.

"Come with us," they said. "We have brought you handsome presents and money from Balak, king of Moab."

"What do you want with me?" Balaam asked.

one felt glad and gay. I said every one felt glad, but I doubt if Balaam did. What do you think about it? Are you *real* happy when you are naughty?

They rode on and on, talking and laughing as they went. Perhaps they sang. People in those days sang when they were on a journey.

The ass Balaam rode was giving him a great deal of trouble. She would not go straight ahead. Once she bolted into a field. Afterwards she ran against a vineyard wall and crushed her master's foot. Balaam was angry and began to beat the poor creature.

After the whipping the ass trotted on obediently, keeping straight in the narrow path. It grew narrower and narrower until it was impossible to turn around. Then she refused to budge another step forward and lay right down in the road. Balaam beat the poor animal again, but she would not rise. Instead, she opened her mouth and spoke to him. And what do you think she must have said? "Why do you abuse me when I have always faithfully carried you?"

Balaam was so enraged that he wanted to kill the poor animal. He was so angry that he was not surprised even to hear the ass speak. This time the wise man was not as wise as his donkey. He did not see the messenger of God standing with drawn sword in the path. The ass had seen the messenger. And the animal had known that she could not go on. Neither could Balaam go on when God's messenger stood in the way.

Some people call God's messengers angels. I think it is a very good name for them, don't you? What do you think Balaam did when at last he saw the angel of the Lord? He fell down, bowing his face to the ground, and promised the messenger to go back to his tent.

"No," said the angel, "you must go on to Moab."

But Balaam was sent there to bless instead of to curse Israel. God was going to put into Balaam's mouth good words and good wishes for the Hebrews. The blessing God sent to Israel through Balaam was a wonderful one. I cannot tell you all of it for you would forget it. But I am going to tell you the part you can remember, and this is it: All people who love and serve God will be helped out of all their troubles. Nothing can hurt them when God is with them. Suppose you and I take that blessing for ourselves.

HOW JERICHO'S WALLS FELL

If you had been down by the river Jordan at the time of our story, I am sure you would have been happy children. So many, many people were camped there. Tents were sprinkled all over the plain. Soldiers were marching up and down the paths between the tents. It was a big camp, almost big enough to be a city. If you had been there I know you would have called it a "tent city." Old men and tiny babies, priests and soldiers, fathers and mothers, and more frolicking, rollicking girls and boys than you could count were in this camp.

Right across the river from the camp was a real city. It was a city with many fine houses and with a great stone wall all around it. The city's name was Jericho.

Can you guess who these people were in the camp by the riverside? Yes, the Hebrews. They had come to the end of their long journey across the wilderness. In the morning they were going to cross the river. Why do you suppose they were so happy to go over the river and camp right beside Jericho? Because Jericho was in Palestine, the country that God had promised to give them. Their good friend Moses was not going over with them. Only a few days before he had gone away from the camp. He had told them that Joshua would lead them across the river and help them to settle in the lovely land lying just beyond it. Moses was an old, old man by the time the people reached the river Jordan. So he went up into a high mountain and looked across the river at the beautiful country into which the Hebrews were going to march.

Moses never came down from that mountain. He stayed with God. Joshua, the warrior, stayed with the people. The Hebrews had so much fighting to do when they entered Palestine that they needed the soldier Joshua with them.

Bright and early in the morning the people started to cross the Jordan. First the priests, then the soldiers and strong men, followed by the mothers and little children. Not a sound did they make, for Joshua had told them they must all keep very still. Soon every one of them had safely crossed the river. Tents were unfolded, camp fires built, the cattle fed, and the little ones laid asleep on goatskin beds. Still no one made a sound. If you had listened with both your ears you would have heard nothing.

The people of Jericho were not friendly toward the Hebrews. They had shut and barred all, the great gates of the city. The very stones in the walls seemed to be saying to the Hebrews, "We don't want you here, keep out!"

But Joshua was determined to get into the city, and he did. How do you suppose he broke down the heavy city walls? Seven priests, each with a ram's horn trumpet, walked slowly around the walls once every day for six days. As they walked they blew those trumpets. You know what a din a small boy can make with a tin trumpet. Just imagine seven strong men blowing on horn trumpets! There must have been some noise. Brave soldiers marched in front of the priests and followed after them.

The people in the tents kept still. For six long nights I don't believe a baby was allowed to cry nor a mother permitted to sing a lullaby. Joshua had said that none but the priests must make a sound until he told them all to shout. And when they shouted they must *all shout together*.

Six days passed away and then came the seventh. The sun was just saying good morning to the hills and shaking the cloud mists out of his eyes when all the people, big and little, walked out of their tents. Every one of them was as quiet as a mouse except the priests, who kept blowing their ram's horn trumpets as they marched around the walls of the city. Once around the city was not enough for the seventh day. On that day the priests, the people, and the soldiers must go around it seven times. I presume the citizens of Jericho thought the Hebrews were all deaf and dumb, because not one of them made a sound. Seven times around Jericho they walked on the seventh day. Then the priests blew a long, loud blast. Before they had finished Joshua called to all the people: "Shout, for Jehovah hath given you the city!"

How they must have shouted after being quiet for six long days! The noise must have seemed louder and stronger than a peal of thunder. You should have seen what happened. Those strong stone walls shook and shivered as though something had struck them. Stones fell from the walls, then flat on the ground fell the great walls themselves. The rich, beautiful city of Jericho belonged to the Hebrews, for all they had to do when the walls fell was to walk in and take it.

STORIES OF GIDEON

THE DEW ON THE FLEECE

All the little boys I know like to play soldier. Most of them want to be captains. And there are some little girls, too, who like to be soldiers and to be captains. One has to be brave and stand up very straight to be a captain. Who ever saw a captain bent over like a hook?

This story is about a soldier who was a captain. His name was Gideon and he was a Hebrew. In his country the people were always fighting. All the Hebrew people were dreadfully afraid of their wicked neighbors. No longer did the poor Hebrews dare to live in their tents and stay in their houses. Many of them had hidden themselves in dark, damp caves, those big holes in the rocks that are always so cold. When their wheat grew tall and was ready to reap, their bad neighbors stole it. When the Hebrews had no wheat they of course could not make flour and could have no bread.

And what do you suppose happened to their clothes? The Midianites, their wicked neighbors, stole their sheep, so the Hebrews could have no warm, woolly sheep-

who were making the Hebrews so unhappy.

Gideon's father and brothers would not help him. They all worshiped idols and they did not love God. Before he could conquer the bad neighbors Gideon would have to do something that would make many of his friends angry. He must throw down every stupid wooden idol. Gideon did not like these idols. He must have thought they were nothing but dolls. Idols look very much like dolls.

Gideon knew Jehovah, the real God, was better than these stupid wooden things. Gideon's bad neighbors, his father and brothers prayed to these idols, but Gideon prayed to Jehovah. That is why the angel visited him.

One very dark night when the moon was playing hide and seek with some black clouds and the stars were too sleepy to shine, Gideon with a few men threw down and broke in pieces every wooden idol.

When morning came the people all gathered together to pray to their idols. But—oh how terribly frightened they were ! Every one of their idols was gone. The people probably expected the sun to fall out of the sky because Gideon had taken those wooden sticks and made a big bonfire of them. Gideon did

skins for blankets or for coats. They were very, very miserable— cold and hungry and homeless.

Gideon would not run away and hide in a cave. He stayed in his father's house. He hid his wheat so that he could make flour out of it. One time when he was threshing his wheat he had a wonderful visitor. Gideon called him the "angel of Jehovah." It was the best kind of a name for the visitor. He had such good news for Gideon that I am sure he must have been an angel. The angel told Gideon that because he was brave and strong God wanted him to go and drive away all the wicked neighbors not want his people to live in caves any longer. The "angel of Jehovah" would help all the Hebrews to live in their tents and houses again if they would stop thinking that silly idols could help them or harm them.

"You must go and drive away your cruel neighbors," the angel had told him. "God is with you and will help you, Gideon."

"Will God give me the victory?" Gideon asked. Then he did a strange thing. He had a beautiful fleece—a soft, woolly sheepskin. I think Gideon had never worn it. When he slept out on the cold hills I do not believe he had ever

used it as a blanket. The fleece must have been very clean and as white as snow. The strange thing Gideon did was to bring out this soft, lovely fleece and lay it on the ground.

Did you ever walk barefoot through the grass early in the morning when every tiny blade of green shone and sparkled with dewdrops? How nice it feels to push your feet through the cool water drops on the grass! Gideon loved the early morning and the glistening dewdrops that came with it. It was nighttime when he put his fleece on the ground. He said, "If there is dew on the fleece in the morning and not a drop on the ground, I shall know that God wants me to

53

go and conquer our bad neighbors." When morning came, there was so much dew on the fleece it glistened as though it were covered with diamonds. But the grass had no dew on it.

"I am going to make one more trial," said Gideon. "Tonight I shall put the fleece out again. If in the morning the fleece is dry and all the grass is wet, I shall be perfectly sure that God wants me to drive away our wicked neighbors, the Midianites."

The fleece was dry in the morning, but sparkling dewdrops glistened on every blade of grass and dripped from every leaf and twig. Gideon was sure now that God wanted him to go. If all those wicked, troublesome Midianites were driven out of the country, the Hebrews would dare come out of their caves and live in their tents and houses again.

Gideon did drive the Midianites away, so far away that they never troubled him any more, nor while he lived did they try to torment the Hebrews. These wandering desert people, the Midianites, who had no homes of their own but who made their living by robbing the homes of others did not want to be whipped again by the brave soldier Gideon.

HOW GIDEON CHOSE HIS SOLDIERS

Gideon must have soldiers. Brave as he was he could not fight battles alone. Where would he get soldiers? From the Hebrew people, of course. They were the ones who had to keep hiding from the troublesome Midianites. When Gideon called for soldiers, out the men marched to meet him. Over the plains, along the riverside, and clambering down steep mountain sides they came.

Each man must have shouted as he ran. In those long-ago days every army had a war cry. When the soldiers all shouted together it made such a noise among the hills that sometimes the enemy army was much frightened and ran away. That saved a great deal of fighting.

Gideon was both wise and brave. He knew that these big, strong soldiers needed something more than powerful muscles. Suppose the great army of the Midianites should frighten them. How much fighting would they do then? Not any that would help win the battle. Gideon meant to win, and his helpers must fight with him. He must choose only brave, really brave, soldiers. He didn't like cowards—some little folks call them "fraidcats"—any more than you or I do. Besides, God is

GIDEON AND THE CAMP OF THE MIDIANITES

with brave people. Those are the people He likes to help.

Gideon wanted his soldiers to learn a lesson. And what do you suppose that lesson was? That it was not strong hands and arms, spears and swords, which gave soldiers the victory. It was only faith in God that really helped them.

Gideon did something queer. His people must have thought he was always doing strange things. I presume they found fault with him and perhaps called him foolish. But his "foolish" acts always turned out to be very wise ones.

The first thing our brave captain did was to send back to his home

every soldier who was afraid. I know you will be surprised when I tell you that more than half of those soldiers decided not to fight. And still Gideon was not sure that every one he still had was a brave soldier. You remember he was hard to satisfy. He always needed more than one sign. He used his beautiful fleece twice before he would believe that God meant him to be a captain. Now he was going to test his soldiers twice before he would lead them to battle.

And this is the strange thing Gideon did after so many of his soldiers had left his army: He asked all who remained to come down with him to the brook. The brook has been called "the spring of trembling." This is just the right name for it, because every man who trembled at this spring was sent home.

It was here Gideon chose all his real soldiers, those who would stick by him and fight till the battle was won. Ten thousand of them went down to the brook. That is more than you can count. The next time you go outdoors at night look up at the sky. You will see it filled with twinkling stars. The men who went with Gideon to the brook were twice as many as the stars we can see.

"Drink," said Gideon to the men. And they did. Some dropped down on their knees. They must have put their faces in the brook and sucked up the water with their lips. Others dipped up the water with their hands and lapped the water from them as a dog laps. Only three hundred of the men drank this way, and these were the three hundred Gideon chose for his soldiers. Do you know why? I suspect Gideon thought those who lapped from their hands had good steady arms which did not tremble from fright. "That is the kind of soldier for me," Gideon must have said. A very, very queer way to choose soldiers, isn't it?

Not so strange does it seem when we stop to think about it. Are all the chubby little girls and boys with strong arms and sturdy legs the brave ones? Not a bit of it! Some very frail little people perform wonderfully brave acts, while some stout looking children tremble all over if a small friendly dog sniffs at their heels.

Gideon wanted to know if his men were really as brave as they looked. He wanted soldiers whose arms never trembled because they were never afraid. Big people or little folks who are easily frightened hinder more than they help.

"I can't be hindered," Gideon must have thought. So the "tremblers" were sent home.

WHAT A DREAM DID FOR GIDEON

The Midianites were making dreadful trouble for everybody and especially for the Hebrews. These Arabs—the Midianites were Arabs— never wanted to live anywhere but in tents. They kept moving most of the time. Skimming across the desert on swift horses or racing on their fleet dromedaries was the only kind of work these Arabs wanted to do. But they needed something to eat and clothes to wear. How could they get these good things if they would not work? From their neighbors who lived in towns, who had houses, and raised wheat and cattle for food. The Hebrews worked and had the good things these fierce Arabs wanted.

So into the Hebrews' country came the Arab robbers. Their

going to try to fight them. God had taught him a better way. And by this better way he was going to save his people from these terrible visitors from the desert.

It must have been a dark, cloudy night with no moon and few stars, when Gideon and his servant, Purah, went softly down the mountain side to visit the Arab camp. The watchmen set to guard the camp were telling each other stories. One Arab soldier had had a strange dream. While he told his dream the soldier and his companion must have been pacing back and forth in the glow of the watch fire. Gideon could see them in the firelight while he and Purah lay still in the shadow of the rocks. Not an Arab knew that brave Gideon was near.

This was the soldier's dream: He had seen a cake of barley bread fall into the Arab camp and this cake had broken down a tent. "That means," exclaimed his listener, "that Gideon is going to destroy our army."

Back went Gideon and Purah; their feet must have had wings on them, they went so fast. Gideon was happy. He had learned that the Arabs were afraid of him. He knew that people who are afraid are easily beaten. Out he called his three hundred warriors. In one hand each of them carried a pitcher with a burning

shabby black goatskin tents were pitched all over the beautiful plain once covered with fields of wheat, fruit trees, and fine fat cattle. The wheat fields of the Hebrews made rich pastures for the Arabs' camels and lean cattle. The Hebrews' goats and sheep were stolen from them in order that the Arabs could have more skins for their tents and warm wool for their clothes.

Gideon was going to drive away these bad neighbors—he, with the three hundred men he had chosen by the brook. When the sun set that night he and his helpers must have peered over the cliffs and looked into the valley below. What a noisy crowd was there! So many camels and so many men that it would take you a whole hour to count them. But Gideon was not torch inside it. In the other hand each one held a trumpet. These trumpets could make a great noise. When they were blown out among the hills it would sound as if there were ten times three hundred trumpets.

Quietly down the mountain side the men crept with Gideon. One hundred of the men went to one side of the Arab camp. Another hundred went to another part of the camp. The three hundred Hebrew warriors made a circle around the Arab camp. Not a sound was heard nor the flash of a torch seen. It was about ten o'clock at night. The Arab robbers probably were asleep. Perhaps some were dreaming about the barley cake. Others may have smacked their lips as they dreamed of the fine fat sheep they would take from the Hebrews the next morning.

Suddenly all around them flashed lights as Gideon's three hundred men smashed their pitchers. The startled Arabs must have thought their whole camp was breaking to pieces. Three hundred trumpets shrieked out in the dark night as Gideon and his men shouted, "For Jehovah and for Gideon!" Then there was a stampede among the Arab army. "Let us run away before we are all killed by these Hebrews," was probably what every Arab was thinking. And run they did.

It was so dark they could not tell an Arab from a Hebrew, so they drew their swords and began to fight one another. The great Arab army killed its own soldiers. Cattle and camels, sheep and goats, were left behind the fleeing Arabs. Tents were torn down as the soldiers rode past on their way back to the desert.

Out from the caves where they had been hiding swarmed the Hebrews, following close after Gideon and his three hundred men who were chasing the frightened Arabs. Down the hills, across the plain, and beyond the river swept the Arab host. Many of them never returned to their desert homes. They were slain by their own swords and by the Hebrew warriors.

Gideon had saved his country.

STORIES OF JOTHAM AND SAMSON

KING OF THE TREES

If you and I were walking on a hot summer day I'm sure each of us would choose the shady side of the road where plenty of big trees were growing. There are so many, many kinds of trees! Tall ones which reach up and prick holes in the clouds and short ones which make us stoop to walk under them. There are some trees whose branches hug tightly to the mother trunk, and others which spread out their boughs and shake their leaves trying to tell people to come and rest under their pleasant shade. Some trees grow tired and sleepy like little folks and are only awake in the summer time, while others keep on their dresses of green needles all the year round like our Christmas tree.

If I should tell you that once the trees wanted a king I know all of you would at once shout: "We know the king of the trees, it is the Christmas tree!" You have all guessed wrong. When the trees chose a king there never had been a Christmas day nor a Christmas tree.

You remember brave Gideon and how he saved the Hebrews from the Midianites. The people afterward asked Gideon to be their king, but he did not want to wear a crown. "God is your king," Gideon told them.

When Gideon died the people were determined to have a king and they elected Abimelech, his son, who was a wicked man. Jotham, another son, good like his father but not so brave, had to run away and hide because the people tried to kill him. But before he hid himself Jotham told the people and his brother Abimelech a story about the trees choosing a king—and here is the story.

The trees wanted a king and went to the Olive tree and asked it to reign over them. The Olive was not a bit pleased by the request. Its rich oil and good fruit which every one enjoyed were much better than being king. "Why should I give up all my fatness whereby I give pleasure to people, just to move my branches over a lot of trees?" the Olive asked.

Although the beautiful Olive had refused to be their king the trees were not discouraged. The Fig tree perhaps would like to be king. But again the trees were mistaken. The Fig tree would

not listen to them. Its delicious fruit fed many hungry people, and giving food to hungry folks was very much better than just waving its branches over a whole forest of trees.

The trees were having a hard time finding a king. No tree that was useful or good for anything wanted to be king. "Let us ask the Vine," they all said. Off to the Vine they went and offered it a royal crown. Think of it! The beautiful Vine bearing luscious grapes from which came sparkling wine! Every Hebrew loved the Vine and wanted one of his own.

The useful Vine scorned being made king as had the Fig and the Olive.

Finally, the only one left for the trees to ask to be king was the ugly, prickly Bramble, and they were foolish enough to choose it. Of course the good-for-nothing Bramble gladly accepted and became king of the trees. "But fire will come out of the Bramble and destroy you," Jotham added when he had finished his story. Then down the mountain side he ran to a place of safety where neither his wicked brother Abimelech nor the foolish Hebrews could reach him.

What a strange story for a man to tell big grown-ups, isn't it? Little children would not be surprised to hear that the trees wanted a king. But big folks know better. Why didn't Jotham tell the pretty parable to the little folks? Because he wanted to teach the Hebrews a lesson. He wanted to show them that they were exactly like the foolish trees when they chose his wicked brother Abimelech for their king. Good Gideon, like the Fig tree, had refused to be king.

Now tell me, all of you, who was the Bramble? Yes, you are right, it was the wicked Abimelech, and wickedness, like a destructive fire, did come out from him and destroyed the foolish Hebrew people who had made him king.

SAMSON: THE SUN MAN

Suppose you and I went walking and looked in at the shop windows. What would you most want to see? Those wonderful walking and talking dolls, and those fine fire wagons with their shiny gongs? We would stop and pick out the prettiest doll and the biggest fire wagon for our very own.

Suppose a big man should come along the street while you and I were looking in at the shop windows. What would you think if he should reach out his hands, pick up the great building, shop and all, and throw it across his shoulders? Then suppose he should march off with it as though it were no heavier than a sack of popcorn. I think your eyes would almost pop out of your head, you would be so astonished.

There once was a man named Samson. Some people called him "Little Sun" because he was so strong. He did very wonderful things—things just as strange as picking up a big store and walking off with it. He never was afraid of anything because nothing was as strong as he. If he were walking in a lonely road and met a hungry lion, do you think that he would run away? No, indeed! Once a savage lion did jump at him.

Samson's strong hands took hold of the wild beast as though it were only a chicken, and tore it apart.

People were afraid of this strong man. It was foolish of them, for Samson did not mean to hurt anyone. He liked to have people see how strong he was, that was all. If people had treated him kindly, he never would have hurt them. But they were not kind; they were cruel. Sometimes when he visited people they bound his hands and arms with heavy rope. It did no good. Samson snapped the rope as though it were only a piece of thread.

One day Samson went into a large city called Gaza. It had high, strong walls around it and thick, heavy gates, or doors, in the walls. Every night these gates were shut and bolted just as we all shut and lock the doors of our houses at night. Our cities, yours and mine, don't have walls around them. The gates of walled cities were large and strong. Some of the gates were so heavy that it took more than ten men to open one gate.

The people who lived in Gaza were sure that their walls were so high and their gates so strong that Samson never would be able to get out of their city. But he played a great joke on them. One night when the people were all asleep and when even the dogs had stopped barking and crawled into their kennels, Samson went down to the city gates. He did not want to stay any longer in Gaza.

The gates were locked. A heavy iron bar was across them. Any one but Samson would have had to wait until morning before he could get out. But not Samson. He put his hands under the great gates, lifted them from their big hinges, and flung them across his shoulders. Then off he started and carried them to the top of a high hill. When the city people awoke in the morning their gates were gone and so was Samson. How the oxen must have pulled and the men shouted when the heavy gates were dragged down the hill and set up in the wall again!

Every one tried to find out what made Samson so strong. A woman named Delilah said she would find out. And she did. Samson foolishly told her that he was strong because he had long hair. One night when he was asleep, Delilah cut off his hair. Poor Samson! As soon as his hair was gone he was weak, so weak that people were able to lock him up in prison. You and I know that if we have our hair cut off it will grow again. Samson's did. The silly people never thought of that. As Samson's hair grew long again he began to be strong.

These wicked people treated him cruelly. They invited him to their feasts but gave him nothing to eat. They only laughed at him and made fun of him.

One day the Philistines had a great feast in the temple of their fish-god, Dagon. They brought Samson in to amuse them. They placed him between the pillars, probably the strong columns which held up the roof. "Let me feel the pillars upon which the house rests," he said to the boy who held his hand. Grasping the two middle pillars he gave them a mighty pull. Down he bowed with all his might as he held the pillars. Crack! Crash! In fell the roof and the temple walls, burying Samson and his tormenters in the ruins.

SAMSON GAVE A MIGHTY PULL. CRACK! CRASH! IN FELL THE ROOF

STORIES OF SAUL AND DAVID

SAUL AND SAMUEL

Did you ever lose anything and have to hunt for it? What a time you had running upstairs and down, turning pockets inside out and boxes upside down, in your efforts to find it!

Our story for today is about a man who had lost something too large to be kept in a drawer or laid carefully away on the shelf—something you couldn't even keep in the house. It was a drove of asses. There is some comfort in hunting for something that will stay in the same place until you can find it. But just think of hunting for something that keeps walking away from you all the time!

That was the work Saul and his servant had to do. Go uphill and down, across fertile meadows and rocky plains, to hunt for his father's asses. If the animals were thirsty they would be down by the riverside. They may have hidden themselves in the woods to get away from the noonday heat. Or, what was annoying to think about, the asses may have broken into somebody's wheat field and be eating the grain. What a bill of damages that would make for Saul's father!

Saul and his servant must have been away from home for a long time, so long that Saul thought his father would surely forget the asses and begin to be anxious about him.

"Let us go home," he said to his servant.

"No," replied the servant, "there is a man in this city who knows everything. Perhaps he can tell us where our asses are."

Saul did not like to ask a favor of "the man of God"—the wise man—without giving him a present. Saul and his servant had eaten all their food and they had nothing else to give the seer. Seers were people who knew a great deal about everything and especially about God.

What should they do? They were far away from home and the seer right in the city near them. It seemed a shame to turn away without consulting the wise man. Saul's servant must have turned the pockets of his belt inside out, for he found some money and told Saul that he had it in his hand.

The city on the hillside must have been a large one, for it had a wall around it. Saul and his servant tramped up the hill to the city gate. There was a well of sparkling, refreshing water close by it. Some girls were drawing water from the well. "Is the seer here?" Saul asked them.

"He is, make haste and enter the city and you will meet him coming out," replied the girls.

Up into the city went the men. And there as they entered the gate was the seer, a beautiful, but sad-looking old man. He was Samuel, the last judge of Israel. He had been expecting Saul all that day. He had never seen Saul, but he knew him at once. Why? Samuel had been wishing for some one who could be king of Israel. All the day before he had prayed that God would send a man to him who could be king. God had answered. He always does answer if our prayers are earnest. When we are earnest we really mean what we say. "Tomorrow about this time I will send thee a man . . . . to be prince

over my people," was the message God sent to Samuel.

And here he was coming straight to Samuel and asking about the asses. Samuel must have been pleased with the strong, powerful body of Saul and thought at once, "Here is the man who will make a fine leader for Israel. He shall be king." Saul did not know that all the time he had been hunting for the lost asses he had been walking toward a crown and a kingdom. We do not always find what we are hunting for, but often we do find something much better. Saul did.

Saul, Samuel, and the servant went up to the very top of the hill and ate their dinner. Samuel had been so sure that the new king was coming that day that he had told the cook to have some especially good meat ready for Saul. He and his servant must have been hungry. Three days they had been away from home with nothing to eat except the food they had carried in their pouches. Dinner was soon over. It was growing late, so they must go down into the city. If they stayed outside until after the sun set the gates of the city would be shut, and all of them would have to sleep on the hills until morning. Where do you suppose Saul did sleep? On the housetop! Strange place, wasn't it? In that hot country people liked to lie on the flat housetops after the sun went down. That was the best place to get the cool night breezes.

Morning time came and off went Saul and his servant. Samuel bade them both good-by. But how he said good-by is another story.

And those lost asses? You do want to know if Saul found them? Yes. Samuel had said to Saul when he met him, "As for thine asses that were lost .... set not thy mind on them; for they are found."

ISRAEL'S FIRST KING

The Hebrews wanted a king. All their neighbors had kings to rule over them. It is all very well for people to be without a king when they live in tents and keep moving all the time. But the Hebrews had stopped wandering about. Many of them had built cities and were living in houses. Some of them owned land and had fruit orchards and wheat fields. The hillsides were covered with olive yards and beautiful vineyards.

The Israelites, who were the Hebrews, were growing rich, and the desert people, roving about like robbers, were always tormenting them. They needed a king to fight their battles. The king and his soldiers could spend their time fighting while the people stayed at home caring for their cattle and their fruitful fields.

One Hebrew did not want a king. He was Samuel, the Judge of Israel, who believed that trusting in Jehovah, God, was better than trusting in a king. Samuel was an old man with long white hair and beard. He had taught the people to do the very things that had made them rich. But the richer the people grew the more wars they had to fight because other countries tried to take their land and their cattle away from them.

Now that Samuel was old the people wanted a king instead of a judge. A king would know much better than Samuel how to fight battles. Do you wonder that Samuel was sad? I do not think he was sorry because the Hebrews wanted a king. They must have some one to rule over them.

Samuel had two wicked sons, so bad that the people would not let them be judges. Now you know why, in our last story, Samuel's face was sad. He must choose a king although he did not want one. He had told the people that it was God and not kings and soldiers who really helped them win. But when folks, big or little, are determined to have their own way sometimes it is best to let them have it.

So Samuel had prayed. No one in Israel prayed as Samuel did. He had asked God to send him a man who could be king and rule over the people. And Saul came. He was God's answer to Samuel's prayer. Saul was handsome. A young man so large and tall that you would have called him a giant. The Hebrews liked big men. Such beauty and bigness they thought must

come from God, so they called Saul "the chosen of the Lord."

Saul was very much surprised to be chosen king. He had cared for his father's asses and had ploughed his father's fields. He was a farmer, really. But a good farmer can also make a strong soldier. The king of Israel must be a soldier, for he would have so much fighting to do. You remember why the Hebrews asked for a king and said: "We will have a king . . . . that our king may . . . . fight our battles." Samuel was not a soldier.

The morning after Saul had slept on the housetop Samuel called him early and sent him home to his father. Samuel and Saul walked down to the city gate together — the sad, disappointed old man and the handsome young giant, Saul. When they reached the gate Samuel did something you would have thought strange. He told Saul to stand still, and then he poured over Saul's head a bottle of oil. Samuel gave him a kiss and called him king.

Poor Samuel! When he anointed Saul as king he expected to guide him as he had guided Israel. He would show Saul how to be a good king. But Saul was like the rest of the Hebrews, he wanted his own way. He loved Samuel and wanted him as a friend, but he did not care enough about him to listen to his advice. The Hebrew people never had but three good kings, and I am sorry to have to tell you that Saul was not one of them.

Samuel must tell the people about their new king and must show him to them before his — Samuel's — work was over. He made a great feast. Every Israelite was invited. Saul came with his family. Every one of his relatives must have been there. Once more Samuel told the Hebrews that they were making a great mistake in asking for a king. Some day they would be sorry and wish they had remembered God and trusted in Him. But the people would not listen to Samuel. They looked at Saul, who was head and shoulders taller than any of them. How proud they were of this grand looking man! Surely he would know how to fight their battles and be able to shout a song of victory. Surely a big man like Saul would always win. The wicked neighbors who were always tormenting and robbing them would now be driven away. The Hebrews came forward and greeted their new king. "Long live the king!" they cried. Saul was now ruler over Israel and Samuel's work was done. The Hebrews had their king.

MAD KING SAUL

Saul was a great fighter. He was big and strong and was not afraid. He led the Hebrews out to battle and drove away many of their bad neighbors. Some of those wicked neighbors came with their camels, their tents, and their chariots and camped on the Hebrews' land. The Hebrews were frightened. They were so afraid that they promised to be servants of those bad neighbors. But the wicked neighbors were spiteful. They were always doing horribly cruel things. The captain of these bad men said to the Hebrews: "If you will let me put out all your right eyes I will make peace with you." Nobody wants to lose an eye. The Hebrews didn't. "Let us think about it for a week," said the Hebrew elders. Off they posted to Saul's home and told him the terrible trouble they were having. Saul was dreadfully angry. How glad he was that he had strong arms! He would go after those bad neighbors and punish them for their wickedness.

I don't believe the wicked neighbors knew the Hebrews had a king who could raise a big army and drive them out of the country. Just imagine the cruel men in their tents sharpening their knives with which they intended to cut out the eyes of the Hebrews. But they never used

those knives. Saul and his soldiers fell upon them and drove them away. Of course the Hebrews shouted with joy. They were sure now that they had been wise in asking for a king.

Poor King Saul! He knew how to fight battles but he did not know how to rule his kingdom. A boy with a pair of skates and no feet is no worse off than was King Saul. He had something—a kingdom—that was only a burden because he did not know enough to take care of it. When you move your hands and your feet those little heads of yours tell you how to do it. Saul had a handsome head but the "thinker" inside of it was always telling him to do things that were wrong.

Saul kept fighting and fighting battles. He grew powerful and his bad neighbors were beginning to be afraid of him. Then something sad happened — so sad that every one who reads about King Saul feels sorry for him. I am much afraid that Saul had forgotten about God, that he trusted in his strong muscles instead of having faith in God. Saul had dreadful spells of being unhappy. When Saul had those gloomy spells he always shut the door of his tent. He wanted to be alone in the dark. While he felt so badly he would not eat or sleep. He was so miserable he would not speak to anyone. You and I are not surprised that Saul had those gloomy spells. No one who forgets God can be happy. Saul really was afraid even of Samuel, the old man who had made him king. Samuel was sorry too. He loved Saul and was bitterly disappointed that the king should do so many foolish things.

Saul surely was growing timid and suspicious — that long word means always thinking people want to harm you. He was so suspicious that he always kept his tall, heavy spear near him. When he ate he held it in his hand. When he slept it lay beside him. Sitting in his tent it leaned against his side.

Saul must have grown vain, for when he went into battle he wore a golden crown on his head and a bracelet on his arm. What hard work it must have been for the King to keep his crown on when he was fighting!

Poor King Saul had one very, very bad spell of being sad. His great, powerful body did not sit straight and strong on his throne. It was limp like a baby's. His head fell over on his breast, his eyes were closed and his mouth open. What a dreadful condition for a great king to be in! He must have moaned and rolled his head from side to side. Do you wonder that his soldiers were frightened? They tried to help him but he seemed only to grow worse. What should they do? King Saul dearly loved music. Perhaps that would help him. They must find some one who could play the harp and sing to him: Then they thought of David out on the sunny hillside singing as he watched his sheep. Would Saul see him? Yes, the king wanted them to send for the boy.

And David came, his sweet face bright and cheery. His kind eyes were full of love for everything. His fingers lightly moved over the harp strings. Instead of the moans of the king the tent was filled with music. The king grew quiet, lifted his head, and listened as the shepherd boy began to sing. It was a most wonderful song. It must have been about the God King Saul had almost forgotten. And it must have been a happy song. The sparkling stars, the golden sunshine, the fresh breezes whispering among the branches, the earth's carpet of grass and beautiful flowers, and the singing birds, all must have been in David's song. The sweet song, low and soft at first, grew higher and stronger as David sang of God, whom he loved best — God who gives to all life and health and strength, God who loves his people and wants them to be happy, God whose presence always leads into the light.

When the song was finished King Saul was well. And now he wanted David always to be near him, so he made him his armor-bearer. The shepherd lad went to live in the king's beautiful palace. And God was with him there. Green hillside or king's palace, gentle sheep or cruel men made no difference in David, for God was the friend he trusted.

GOD'S ANOINTED

Samuel must choose a new king. He felt sorry about it, but he saw that poor mad King Saul was not a good ruler for Israel. He had loved Saul and had chosen him for king because he was big and strong and a fine fighter. I think Samuel must have asked God to send him a brave soldier. And the brave soldier, Saul, had come, but he had not made a good king. Once more Samuel talked with God. He was foolish to keep grieving about Saul instead of looking for a new king.

I do not believe Samuel asked God for a soldier this time. I think he did not even wish the new king to be big and powerful. He was beginning to see as God saw. "Jehovah seeth not as man seeth; for man looketh on the outward appearance, but Jehovah looketh on the heart."

There was a man named Jesse who lived in a little town called Bethlehem. This man had many sons. Jesse belonged to the tribe of Judah, a lot of strong, true, brave men. God sent Samuel to Jesse to see his sons. At first he was afraid to go. Suppose Saul should hear that he had visited Jesse in order to choose a new king. Saul would try to kill Samuel. But it was not wise to wait.

KING SAUL LISTENING TO DAVID'S SONG OF GOD

Every day Samuel was growing older and more feeble and Saul was growing worse. Samuel must not leave Israel with such a king.

It was the time of the yearly festival in Bethlehem. Samuel would go to this feast, take the people a young heifer, and keep the feast with them. No one would suspect his errand. While they were gathered about the feast Samuel intended to see all Jesse's sons and choose one of them for king. Samuel was only going to anoint the young man. He did not intend to tell him he had been chosen. When Saul had been made king so much had been done for him that it had spoiled him. The new king was only going to be chosen. After that he must win his throne and show he deserved it. That is the best way. Big people and little people

who work for what they receive know better how to take care of it.

Everything was ready for the feast. Jesse and his seven stalwart sons were waiting for Samuel to speak. "Why does he carry that flask of oil?" Jesse must have thought. Samuel asked to see the young men, one at a time. Up started Eliab, the eldest, and walked slowly past Samuel.

Jesse must have said to himself: "If the prophet has come for one of my sons he surely will choose Eliab." For a moment that was exactly what Samuel did think as he looked admiringly upon Eliab's broad shoulders and tall stature. But only for a moment did he think it. Into Samuel's heart came the knowledge that God chose men because of their hearts and not because of their looks.

Back into his leathern pouch Samuel slipped the flask of oil. Eliab was not the future king. Two more of Jesse's sons passed before the prophet. All were big fine fellows, fearless soldiers in Saul's army. At last he had seen the seven sons, and still the flask of anointing oil lay in his pouch. Samuel hesitated. "He has seen my seven sons," thought Jesse, "and none has pleased him. Why does he stay?"

Samuel spoke, saying: "Are here all thy children?"

"I have one more," said Jesse. "He is the youngest and keeps my sheep." In those days that was just the same as saying, "He does not amount to much; it is foolish to ask for him." In that long-ago time nobody tended sheep except slaves, the girls of the family, and those boys the family cared little about.

"Send for him," commanded Samuel. David, the shepherd boy, came. Then Samuel drew the flask of oil from his pouch, for he knew Israel's future king stood before him. Jesse, David's seven brothers and the people were gathered around the feast which none had tasted. Samuel would not eat until David appeared. Among the little group stood the sweet-faced shepherd lad. The light of a brave, strong spirit shone in his eyes. The tone of his voice showed that he was fearless and true. "Here is power and sweetness," Samuel must have thought. Then on David's head the prophet poured the anointing oil. He was God's chosen.

David knew he had been set apart for something, but what it was he did not know, for Samuel never told him. Samuel left the lad in God's hands. The prophet did not intend to do David's work for him. Samuel had tried to do that for Saul and had failed. Now David, led by God's spirit, must show that he had a right to be king.

Soon after, David went for a time to live with Saul. When Saul had

dreadful sad spells then David soothed him with his music. At first no one knew that David was a fighter. He did not look like one. But way down deep in his heart was a spirit that never intended to be beaten at anything. Saul and his soldiers discovered that David could win battles and frighten away the enemy. One time David won a great victory. On his way home some women sang to Saul and to his soldiers: "Saul hath slain his thousands, and David his ten thousands." Saul was very angry to hear this song, and from that hour he hated David and tried to kill him. During all his life he tried to harm David. But he could not hurt him, for David was to be the next king. God had anointed him.

THE FLIGHT OF AN
ARROW

It was very fortunate for Israel — the Hebrews — that the king had a son as good as Saul was evil. Jonathan was his name. He was big and strong like his father but in spirit he was like David. A boy or girl like that is sure to win. Jonathan did. He started out, with only his armor-bearer to fight the Philistines. All these wicked neighbors had swords and spears. And their swords and spears were keen and sharp. Jonathan had the same weapons but they were not good for anything. How do we know they were not? Because the people who knew how to sharpen the edges of swords and the points of spears all lived with the Philistines. Of course the Philistines did not allow their smiths to sharpen the swords and spears of their enemies, the Hebrews. So in the Hebrews camp, wherever there was a sword or spear, it must have been dull and blunt, not keen and sharp.

The Philistines did not do much thinking or they would have remembered an important thing about Jonathan, Saul's son. In Israel and outside of it every one knew that Jonathan was a great archer. An archer is one who knows how to use a bow and arrow. Jonathan's bow must have been nearly as tall as himself. It was strong and able to send heavy arrows a long distance. And those arrows were cruel weapons, tipped as they sometimes were with poison, or else with something on their points which stung and burned like a hot coal. It was said that Jonathan never missed any object at which he aimed. No one ever wanted to get in his way when he had his bow and arrows with him.

The Philistines had been frightening the Hebrews dreadfully, so much so that many had left their homes and were hiding in caves and holes in the rocks. Some of the poor Hebrews had been stolen away from their people and made to work in the Philistine camp.

How those wicked neighbors of the Israelites must have laughed as they watched King Saul's army on the opposite hill! Not a soldier dared attack the Philistines. How could men do so without swords and spears? The Philistines were so busy laughing at Saul's weak army that they did not see two men climbing up their hill. You and I know who those two men were — the powerful archer, Jonathan, and his brave armor-bearer.

Up and up the two men clambered along the steep side of the hill. The path must have been slippery with loose stones. Jonathan was a good climber and could use his hands as well as his feet when he scrambled over the rocks. His armor-bearer was close beside him, for if Jonathan was not afraid he was not going to be. Their bows were slung over their shoulders and their quivers filled with arrows hung across their backs.

Jonathan intended to surprise the Philistines. Often when people are surprised they are frightened. Jonathan thought the Philistines

would be, and they were. But I am getting ahead of my story. And it is never wise to be in too great a hurry when one is telling a story.

"Jehovah can save with a few as easily as he can with many," said Jonathan to his armor-bearer. If God was with them then they need have no fear. Jonathan and his helper both believed that God was with them, but each wanted a sign. If only something would happen that would show them exactly what they should do! And that something did happen.

The Philistines peering over the rocks saw them coming. With yells and shouts these wicked neighbors

greeted the two men. "Look at those Hebrews coming out of their holes in the rocks to look at us," they screamed. The soldiers jeered at Jonathan and his armor-bearer. What could those two men do without sword or spear? They were very soon to find out what the two archers could do. "Come up to us and we will show you a thing," shouted the Philistines.

With a great leap and a bound Jonathan landed in the midst of the Philistine camp, his armor-bearer close beside him. The Philistines were so surprised they did not move. Before they could draw their swords Jonathan's arrows flew thick and fast upon them. If the Philistines ran, those dreadful arrows followed and pinned soldier after soldier to the ground. The poisoned points and stinging tips never missed their mark. As arrow after arrow whistled through the air the Philistines must have screamed aloud with pain and fright. Down the hill they ran with Jonathan and his armor-bearer after them. The Philistines must have been blinded by the sting of the arrows, for when they did draw their swords they began to slay one another.

Out from the caves and from behind the rocks where they had hidden, swarmed the Hebrews. The Hebrew prisoners in the Philistine camp escaped from their captors and followed after Jonathan and his armor-bearer. Flying down the opposite hill came King Saul and his army, all of them anxious to help the brave Jonathan and his noble armor-bearer. God had saved Israel by the flight of an arrow. The Philistines had fled before it.

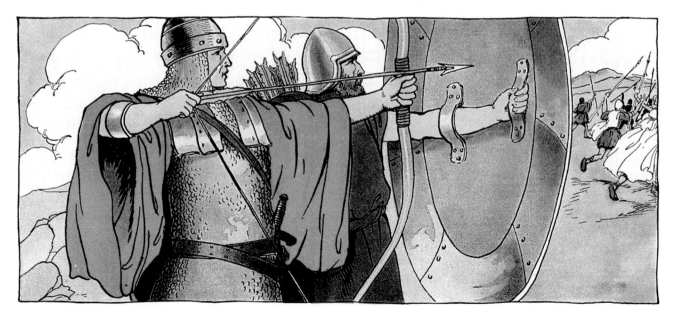

HONEYCOMB

Soldiers get very hungry. Tramping through the mud, wading across shallow streams, climbing steep hills, and cutting their way through dark forests make them also very tired. Sometimes they must sleep outdoors in the pelting rain. All these things together give them little chance to be comfortable. Something to eat is about the only pleasant thing that comes into a soldier's life. The soldier fights better when he has plenty of food. No one with an empty stomach feels lively. Saul's army did n't.

After Jonathan and Saul's army had chased the Philistines away the men were hungry and tired. How wise it would have been if Saul had given his soldiers a hearty meal! All the men were feeling miserable, no doubt gloomy and discouraged, as hungry people often are. Saul noticed it. If he had had as much sense as Jonathan, his son, he would have had pity on his men and fed them. Instead, he must have been afraid — Saul spent most of his time being afraid of something — that the soldiers would desert him. So he made a cruel and wicked vow. Any man who ate even a morsel of food before night was to be put to death. I

suppose Saul thought the soldiers were so hungry that they would be sure to follow him because they expected something to eat at the close of the battle.

So on the tired army marched. Jonathan was ahead but they soon reached him. Jonathan was tired too. And he was dizzy with hunger. He had worked even harder than the other soldiers, for Jonathan and his armor-bearer alone had routed the Philistines. They all entered a deep cool, forest. How grateful the shade must have been after the long march under the hot sun! No doubt they wished to stop and drink at some of the cool, refreshing brooks that hurried through

the forest. Suddenly buz-z-z buz-z-z sounded in their ears. What was it? A great swarm of bees. And that meant delicious honey. The exhausted men, faint with hunger, looked around them. In the hollows of the tree trunks and dripping upon the ground was a mass of rich, yellow honey. How the men must have smacked their dry lips! Plenty of honey for all of them and none dared touch it! They were afraid of Saul's cruel vow. Jonathan had not heard his father's vow. He did not know why the half-starved soldiers did not eat the honey which God had provided.

Jonathan dipped his staff in the luscious honey and ate some of it. He felt better at once.

"Your father has forbidden us to eat," said a soldier.

"My father is hurting the army," replied Jonathan. "If the men had been given something to eat then they would have slain more of the Philistines." Jonathan knew that soldiers who have rested and have had some food fight better and win more battles.

Night came. It was dark in the forest. Not a sound was to be heard except the twitter of some sleepy bird or the noise of some small animal rustling through the underbrush. "Let us go down and destroy all the Philistines and take all their goods," said Saul. The soldiers agreed but not one moved. "What hinders us?" asked Saul. "Some one has sinned," he added. All the soldiers must be questioned to find out which one of them had done wrong that day. Not one of them could be blamed for anything.

At last Jonathan stood before his father, the king. "What have you done?" anxiously inquired Saul.

"I have eaten honey," Jonathan replied.

Yes, faint and weak, he had eaten the honey and had felt better. He had been sorry for the hungry soldiers, and had wanted them to have the food which they deserved. The king had been cruel in his vow, so Jonathan had told the soldiers. What do you suppose Saul did when he discovered Jonathan was the culprit? Did he say: "This time we will not keep the vow?" Indeed, not! In those days and among those people when a vow was made it had to be kept. They believed in keeping a promise although it was a wicked one.

"Jonathan must die," declared Saul. The army heard his words. Was every soldier glad that he had escaped and that it was the king's son who was guilty of disobeying Saul's command? "What, destroy Jonathan!" cried every one of them. "Put to death the brave man who has saved Israel?" I can see the flashing eyes of the soldiers, can see all of them raise their bows and cruel arrows, or poise their slings in readiness to hurl the deadly stones at the first man who dared touch Jonathan. "There shall not one hair of his head fall to the ground; for he hath wrought with God this day," shouted the army in unison. Saul dared not keep his insane vow. Jonathan was saved because the army had seen that God was with the brave archer of Israel.

TWO MARKSMEN

Jonathan the great archer and brave soldier loved everything that was great. He admired courage in other people. He probably was glad whenever he could praise one of his soldiers for being brave. Because he was brave and true God sent Jonathan a friend— a man like himself, of course. A hero and a coward cannot be friends. Besides, this friend needed Jonathan's help. That is why God sent him to Jonathan. Who do you suppose this friend was? David, the shepherd lad.

Jonathan's bow was powerful. So was David's sling. Neither Jonathan's bow nor David's sling ever missed the mark at which they were aimed. Each had a clear eye and a perfect aim. David had gone out alone, without wearing any heavy armor, and had slain a powerful giant with his sling, a giant who had made every Hebrew quake with fear. Goliath, the giant, was a Philistine. I have no doubt that he walked up and down before the Hebrew soldiers and shook his fist in their faces. Even Saul the king was afraid of Goliath. When David slew the savage giant, Goliath, with his sling all the troublesome Philistines were driven away again.

"Who is the lad?" Saul asked the captain of his army. "I do not know," replied the captain. David answered Saul's question himself, for he came to the king's tent as soon as he had slain the giant. He told Saul that he was only a shepherd lad, the youngest son of an old man named Jesse, who lived in Bethlehem. Jonathan was watching as Saul and David talked together. The more he looked at the frank-faced boy the more he loved him. Could you and I have known what Jonathan was thinking as he watched David I'm sure it would have been this: "There is a strong spirit, he is brave and true, God must be with him." From that day Jonathan and David were friends.

Every one with the spirit of love in his heart wishes to give. Jonathan

did. He admired David's spirit; and how do you think he showed it? In those days people showed their respect for another by taking off their upper garment and giving it to the one they loved. David, you know, was only a shepherd. Jonathan was a prince, the son of a king. He took off his robe and put it on David. He gave David his sword, his wonderful bow, and his girdle, which was Jonathan's way of saying: "You are as much a prince as I."

King Saul was not like his son Jonathan. What pleased the great archer made the mean and selfish soul of Saul jealous. Saul wanted to love David; he even tried to do so many times. But he was afraid of the shepherd lad who was also a brave soldier and beloved by all the people. Saul was afraid of losing his kingdom. Samuel had told him that he would lose it. Who the next king would be no one, not even Saul or David, knew. Samuel knew but he did not tell. Saul was dreadfully frightened as he watched David win battle after battle with the Philistines. I know he must have said to himself after every victory: "This David no doubt is the next king." So the king hated the shepherd lad and often tried to kill him.

Saul had another of those dreadful sad spells. Again David sang and

DAVID, THE SHEPHERD LAD AND GOLIATH, THE GIANT

played for him. Saul this time was not helped. His heart was so filled with rage and jealousy that he hurled his spear at David. It missed David and struck the wall. Saul was trying to take everything away from David, even his life. But David's wonderful friend Jonathan, the archer of Israel, gave everything he had to David. It made Jonathan sad to see how his father hated David. He was not even jealous when he thought that David might be king instead of himself. The more you know of Jonathan the better you will love him and you will be glad that David had this friend to help him when Saul made David's life so unhappy.

WARNED BY AN ARROW

There were four places at Saul's table, and who do you suppose sat in them? First came King Saul, his spear near him and a golden crown on his head. Beside him was Abner, captain of the king's army. Jonathan and David were the other two. Jonathan always carried his bow with him and surely David must have had his harp. King Saul so often was disturbed by his sad, angry spells that David must keep the harp near by so that he could soothe him with its sweet music. Such a happy group it might have been! But it was not, because one of the company had an ungoverned, jealous temper. One person can make many people miserable. Saul did. He hated David but he could not get along without him, and this made him all the angrier.

Every servant in King Saul's house had been told to kill David. Poor King Saul! He surely had a sick mind. His strong, powerful body did not help him because the "thinker" in his head so often went wrong. Once he had been gentle and kind, but now he hated and wanted to kill. It was David, his son's friend, whom he most hated.

"Why," Jonathan asked his father, "do you wish to hurt David?

You saw him deliver Israel from the giant and the Philistines, and you were glad," Jonathan added. For a little while Saul was ashamed of himself. Then David won another battle with the wicked Philistines which again made the king savage. Nothing that David did pleased Saul. "David must die, David must die, or I shall lose my kingdom," Saul must have been thinking to himself all the time.

"What have I done that your father should hate me?" David asked Jonathan. The archer did not know. He said to David: "Nothing shall harm you for I will protect you." And Jonathan kept his word.

When David ate at Saul's table I wonder if he did not wish he were out on the green hills again watching the gentle sheep and frisky lambs? It surely would have been much safer. The lion and the bear he had met on those lonely hills were not half as terrible as the savage king. As David ate he must have watched the glistening spear so close to Saul's cruel fingers— that wicked spear which was so often hurled at David. The spear meant death for David. The bow and arrows of the archer, Jonathan, were to bring David life. How? That is what our story is going to tell us.

"I shall not eat dinner with you tomorrow," David had told Jonathan. "I do not feel safe with your father," he added. Dinner time came. Saul, Jonathan, and Abner were there but David's place was empty.

The next day also David was absent. Saul was furious. "Where has that lad gone?" he raved. Jonathan said David had gone to see his brothers. Saul did not believe it. He was afraid that Jonathan had helped David to escape. The king spoke terrible words to Jonathan, he called him and his mother evil names. "Why do you make this son of Jesse your friend?" Saul asked. "Don't you know that as long as David lives you will never be king?" Jonathan did know but he did not

care. He would like to be king, of course. He was the prince and had a right to be king after his father died. But Jonathan loved something better than he loved being king. He loved to do right, and he knew it was not right to kill David. Besides, he loved David and had promised to help him. Jonathan never intended to desert his father nor was he going to allow Saul to harm his friend. Jonathan meant to do his best for both of them.

When Saul flew into a rage at dinner because David was absent, Jonathan asked him, "What has David done that he should be put to death?" The furious king answered by seizing his spear and hurling it at Jonathan. It missed him. Saul's spear seemed always to be missing its mark. His rage and jealousy must have blinded him so that he could not see to throw straight. The archer angrily left the table.

For a whole day Jonathan ate nothing he was so grieved about David. Before that he had not believed Saul intended to kill his friend. But now he knew David was not safe in Saul's house. He was not even safe in the country where Saul lived. Jonathan must warn his friend and help him to escape from the savage king.

What should Jonathan do? How could he see David and tell him to flee for his life? Not a hard matter for the archer of Israel. His arrows had won battles. They had brought down everything at which they had been aimed, whether it was bird, beast, or wicked Philistine. Now his arrows should carry a message. The next time Jonathan shot them from his bow it would not be to kill. The next time his arrows whizzed through the air they would carry a warning to the waiting David. How? David and Jonathan had planned beforehand how it should be done. Saul, even if he had been there watching, would never have suspected what the arrows were saying.

David was hiding in a field. In that country it is always very easy to hide. There are so many rocks behind which one can crouch or caves into which one can crawl. It was morning, the sun shone and the birds sang. The little lad who trotted by Jonathan's side must have whistled for joy. It was such a beautiful day in which to be happy. But Jonathan's heart was heavy. His arrows today were going to do the saddest work they had ever been asked to do. They were going to send David, the friend he loved as his own soul, away from him forever. But the archer did not hesitate; he must act quickly for his friend's safety.

He paused beside a great rock. No one but Jonathan knew that David was hiding behind that huge rock. Jonathan drew his bow to his shoulder and an arrow sped over the field, then another and another till three arrows lay together upon the ground. "Go fetch me the arrows," Jonathan said to the little lad who was with him. As the boy reached the arrows Jonathan called to him in a loud voice: "Is not the arrow beyond thee?—make speed, haste, stay not." David, listening behind the rock, knew what those words meant; they had really been meant for him instead of for the boy. The

message the arrows had carried told David that his life was not safe with Saul. The king intended to kill him. He must go.

"Take the arrows to the city," Jonathan said to the little lad. He went. Jonathan was alone. Then from his hiding place came David. The two friends kissed each other and wept. Jonathan had kept his word and saved his friend. "Go in peace," Jonathan said to David. "Jehovah shall be between me and thee—forever." David turned to go. He must leave home, friend, and country. His life was spared, but until Saul, the king, was dead he was hunted from place to place as a cat hunts a mouse.

A FRIENDLY ENEMY

David, the morning Jonathan sent him away went to Ahimelech the priest. The priest was afraid, when he saw David for it was dangerous to be kind to him. Saul had said David must be killed. Saul intended to murder any person who treated David kindly. But Ahimelech was a good man and gave the hungry lad some bread. He did more: he let David have Goliath's great sword.

Some people seem to have eyes in the back of their heads and are able to see all around them at once. Saul did. Not real eyes, of course, but something that served him just as well as a second pair of eyes. Suppose we call Saul's chief herdsman, Doeg, a pair of eyes for Saul. This wicked man's eyes watched David and the priest. Did he have pity for them? Not a bit! Off Doeg hurried to tell the savage king.

Poor David, no place was safe for him! When he went into the desert Saul crossed the hot sands after him. If he sought shelter in the cool forest, he soon heard the tramp of Saul's soldiers and knew that he must find another place where he could hide. There were other men besides David who had to run away from the king. All these men banded together and chose David as their leader. He must have been happier when he had companions. David and his men hid in dark, damp caves. Those gloomy places were often filled with darting bats, gliding snakes, and ugly spiders. When they fled to the desert they would find little to eat. They might have been fortunate enough to find ostrich eggs hidden in the sand. Night time in the forest was not more pleasant. Hooting owls, barking foxes, and yelping jackals must have disturbed the men. Bears were in the mountains and wolves were on the plain, but David and his men knew it was safer to live with the wild beasts than to be near savage King Saul.

Saul, all out of breath from hunting David for so long, sat down under a tree to rest. He was angry with his servants and his soldiers. He told them they were not sorry for him, that they were helping David to escape. "My son Jonathan has joined hands with David and now both are against me," complained the king.

Up spoke Doeg the herdsman, the wicked fellow who watched David and the priest. Then this miserable creature, who was Saul's second pair of eyes, told the king about David's visit and Ahimelech's kindness. I wonder that his words did not choke him. "Send for Ahimelech," cried Saul. Ahimelech came and many other priests came with him.

"Kill every priest," commanded the king. But the soldiers did not raise a bow to their shoulders nor put a stone in their slings. The soldiers respected the priests and would not touch them. The furious king then shouted to Doeg, "Turn thou and fall upon the priests." Worse than the wild beasts was this savage Doeg. He drew his sword and slaughtered all the priests. This terrible man did another awful thing. He went to the priests' city and killed every one in it, except Abiathar one of Ahimelech's sons. Men, women, little children, all were killed. Not an ox, an ass, nor a sheep was left alive.

Then Jonathan came to see David. He wanted to keep the shepherd lad from being discouraged. "Don't be afraid, my father will never be able to find you," said Jonathan. He

knew his father was a bad king and that David would make a good king. Israel ought to have a good king, so Jonathan told David that some day he would be king. Samuel had known all the time that David would be king, but he had told no one. "You have promised to be kind to my children when you are king," added Jonathan. Then back to his house went the faithful friend and David turned into the wilderness.

David and his men were asleep in their cave. Something startled them and they awoke. They saw Saul alone groping his way into the dismal cavern. The king sat down to rest. "Now is your chance," whispered David's men. "Your enemy is here in your power; kill him." David reached forth his hand but drew it back.

"I cannot kill him, God has anointed him king," David answered. He crept softly behind Saul and cut off the skirt of his long robe. Soon Saul left the cave with David following him. When the king was at a safe distance David called to him and said: "See the skirt of your robe which I have cut! You were in my power and I did not kill you. God will deliver me out of your hand."

Saul was ashamed; for a moment he was sorry he had been so wicked. "God will reward you because you have not killed me," Saul said to David. Then he cried out, "I know well that thou shalt surely be king." Saul asked David not to destroy his family. David promised. The king went back to his camp, and David and his men left the cave, that they might to be farther away from Saul. The mad king could not be trusted.

THE SONG OF THE BOW

Saul's old enemies, the Philistines, were wide awake. They were all improving every minute of their time getting ready to march into the Hebrews' country and steal it away from them. The Philistines were envious of the Israelites because they wanted their rich country. What was Saul doing? Wasting his time hunting David until he drove the brave captain and his men out of the country. The Philistines were afraid of David because he always whipped them whenever they ventured into the land of Israel, and sent them running back into their own country.

David had gone. Samuel was dead. And Jonathan's arm must have grown weak. His grief over his friend and Saul's savage temper must have made it so. "Now is our time to invade the Israelites' country," the Philistines must have said. And into it marched the Philistine army. Saul saw it coming and his knees knocked together with fright. The long lines of glittering spears, the powerful archers with their great bows, the prancing horses and heavy chariots of the Philistines made Saul's heart sick with fear. He looked at his own miserable little army. What could his handful of soldiers do against the thousands of mighty warriors camped beside him in the valley? King Saul had no horses nor chariots, his swords and his spears were dull. What was worse than all, the king, his soldiers, and all his people were dreadfully frightened. I think all of them must have been thinking more of where they could hide than of how they could fight.

King Saul needed help. Where would he get it? He had killed the priests and had driven away the prophets. He tried to pray. He must have forgotten how, because God, Jehovah, did not answer him. Something must be done, and at once, for tomorrow was to be the great battle with the Philistines.

The king's servants told him there was a witch in Endor. "Let us visit her tonight, perhaps she can help you," some of them suggested. And Saul and two of his men went to talk with the witch. This showed that he had forgotten God.

The black night hid their journey from Gilboa, Saul's camp, to the witch's cave in Endor. Saul and his two men hurried along the path. It was many miles to Endor and the road was rough and stony and full of holes, but they traveled along in the dark until they reached the witch's home. They must have ridden on donkeys, for those little

animals can find their way in the dark. King Saul had tried to drive every witch and wizard out of his kingdom. Perhaps they may have kept telling the people that David was going to be king. Only the old woman in Endor was left, and she had bad news for him.

"Call Samuel for me," Saul said to the woman.

"I see an old man covered with a robe," she replied.

All was still. The fluttering of the leaves and the croaking of the frogs must have hushed as Saul cried, "It is Samuel!"

"Why do you call upon me?" inquired Samuel.

"God has departed from me," Saul replied.

"I have no power to help you if God has departed from you," Samuel replied.

Saul could not answer. He could only listen as Samuel uttered the terrible words that told the king his punishment was near at hand.

"You have lost your kingdom and it will be given to David," Samuel said. And he added, "The Philistines will conquer Israel, and tomorrow you and your sons will die on the battlefield."

King Saul fell upon the ground. All his mighty strength left him. The witch tried to comfort him, and coaxed him and his men to eat. Then out into the night they went, back to Gilboa.

With the morning came the battle. The frightened Hebrews ran wildly in every direction. Arrows whizzed through the air. Swords flashed, and chariot wheels ground under them the bodies of Hebrew soldiers. Jonathan lay dead upon the hill— the great archer of Israel had fallen before the archers of the Philistines. Jonathan's two brothers lay dead beside him. The wounded king leaned heavily upon his sword. "Kill me before the Philistines take me prisoner," Saul begged his armor-bearer. The young man dared not obey, for he was afraid to harm the king. Saul flashed his sword in the air, fell upon it, and its blade pierced through his body. The armor-bearer then fell upon his sword, and king and squire died together.

* * * * * * * * *

A courier from the battlefield brought David the news. David mourned, he and his men. All day they wept and fasted. In a song David told the love he 'had for Jonathan. Every child in Judah was taught this song and the use of the bow. David did not wish his faithful friend forgotten, so he made it a rule in Judah that the children should remember the great archer by learning archery.

Here is the song which David sang about Jonathan:

> " From the blood of the slain, from
>   the fat of the mighty,
>   The bow of Jonathan turned not
>   back."
>   * * * * * * *
> "How are the mighty fallen in the
>   midst of the battle!
>   O Jonathan is slain upon thy high
>   places."
> " I am distressed for thee, my brother
>   Jonathan:
>   Very pleasant hast thou been unto
>   me:
>   Thy love to me was wonderful,
>   Passing the love of women."

KING SAUL AND THE WITCH OF ENDOR

KING DAVID

King Saul was dead. He could no longer trouble David nor drive him and his brave soldiers from their homes. I should like to have been in the city of Hebron when David and his big family returned. It was a happy return for David because his clansmen, the men of Judah, anointed him their king. But Judah was only a small part of Israel. The biggest part of it belonged to Ishbosheth, Saul's son. Ishbosheth wanted every bit of the country. He was greedy like his father. But David did not care. If Saul's family wanted to reign over part of Hebrew land he was willing they should. But Joab, the general of David's army, and Abner, Saul's old general, wanted to quarrel. Joab thought David ought to be king and have everything, while Abner was determined Ishbosheth should reign. So David's brave men and Saul's old soldiers kept fighting nearly all the time. In every battle David's men won.

The Philistines were watching and thought it would be easy for them to trouble Israel again. Being king did not seem to give David any rest. Now of course he did not have to keep running away and hiding all the time from savage Saul, but he did have to keep fighting Abner, Saul's general. Besides, he had to send his soldiers many, many times to drive the Philistines out of the country. This was discouraging work, for just as soon as those troublesome neighbors were driven out of one place they came in at another.

The Philistines, always doing dreadful things, had nailed Saul's and Jonathan's bodies to a wall. They were not going to allow the king and Prince Jonathan to be buried. You remember the people Saul once saved from having their right eyes put out? These people were grateful. When all was still at night they stole to the wall and took down the bodies. Saul and his sons were buried by these brave men. This act pleased David. He promised always to be kind to these men because they had treated their dead king and dead prince kindly.

Very different was the fate of the soldier who stole Saul's bracelet and golden crown after Saul had fallen upon his sword. So anxious was this soldier to tell David what he thought would be good news that he ran all the way from the battlefield to David's home. He was so sure King David would rejoice over Saul's death that he told a falsehood. He said he himself had killed Saul. He must have expected a fine present from David or perhaps some money for bringing him the news. Instead he was greatly disappointed, for David had him punished. To kill a king was a crime in David's eyes.

David really was kind-hearted. He wanted to please God. Pleasing God is doing everything as it ought to be done, and that is what David wished to do. But he had a hard time doing it. Many of his people, his soldiers, and even his general, Joab, intended to have their own way, whether it was right or wrong. Do you know any girls or boys like that?

Ishbosheth, thankless like Saul, his father, made his good friend Abner, his father's general, very angry. Instead of praising Abner for helping him to be king, Ishbosheth found fault with him. "There is no use trying to help Saul's family," Abner must have said. "Except Jonathan, they are all greedy and selfish." Ishbosheth was dreadfully frightened when Abner said he was through helping him and now was going to let David have the kingdom. "Jehovah hath sworn to David that he shall be king, and I am not going to fight for you any longer," Abner told him.

Off rushed some messengers from Abner to David. "I am on your side now," Abner wrote to David. "If you will be friendly with me I will make all Israel ask you to be their king." Abner kept his word with David. He saw now that Saul's sons were not the right kind of men to make good kings. The elders of Israel were glad to

have a new king, one whom they could trust. So when Abner said to them, "In times past ye sought for David to be king over you; now then do it." They made David king.

Then David made a great feast for Abner. He liked Saul's old general. You remember about the four places at Saul's table where Saul, Jonathan, Abner, and David sat? I think David and Abner must always have been good friends. Each was brave and strong, and neither one did small, mean things. Abner was open and honest, not false and treacherous, like Joab. David promised Abner that he and all his staff should be safe when they visited Hebron. It was a happy feast. Every one was satisfied. For a long time all the people had really wanted David for their king.

Joab was not present at the feast. He was not in the city when Abner came nor when he and his men left for their homes. Then there happened so wicked and terrible a thing that Joab almost lost his place as David's general. David had promised safety to Abner. Joab was angry. He did not care what David had promised. Joab went after Abner, called him back to Hebron, pretended to be his friend, and while they were talking together Joab stabbed Abner until he died.

What did King David do? He mourned for Abner, and went in the great funeral procession to his grave. David sang a song about Abner as he had about Jonathan. All Israel saw it was Joab's wicked, jealous temper that had made him kill Abner. David was not to blame.

Another thing made David sad. Some bad men wondered why David did not kill Ishbosheth. They kept thinking about it until they themselves decided to kill him. At noonday Ishbosheth lay on his bed asleep. He was trying to rest from the dreadful heat. While Ishbosheth slept these wicked men killed him and hurried to David to tell him of their deed. David was horrified. "Wickedly murdering a man when he was helpless and asleep!" exclaimed David. "You deserve to die yourselves," he added. So David ordered them to be put to death.

"Then came all the tribes of Israel to David, . . . saying . . . In times past, when Saul was king over us, it was thou that leddest out and broughtest in Israel and Jehovah said to thee . . . Thou shalt be prince over Israel." So all the elders came to Hebron and anointed David their king. From all over the country the people traveled to do honor to David. Three times had he been anointed king; that is, he was anointed of God. He surely must have deserved his kingdom. Samuel, the judge of Israel, had seen that David was God's choice. The men of Judah also saw it. At last all Israel knew that God was with David, and they also anointed him their king. The right kind of king, one who knows how to take care of his kingdom, is the only kind of king God ever chooses.

Let us watch the great company of people who came to Hebron when David was crowned. From east and west, north and south, they came. From far away and from homes close by the people flocked to Hebron. There must have been music, dancing, and singing. And the feasting was much like ours on

Thanksgiving Day. Tramp, tramp, tramp came the soldiers of Israel. Shining shields, glittering spears, and flashing swords shone bright in the sunshine as the army crossed the swift Jordan and mounted the hills toward Hebron. The archers of Benjamin followed with their great bows and arrows. Long caravans of happy people brought David presents. Camels and asses were laden with bread. Oxen and mules carried meal, fig-cakes, raisins, oil, and wine. Cattle and sheep the people brought with them, for at this anointing feast they must have plenty of meat. David was king, chosen by his people because he had first been chosen by God.

THE LITTLE LAME PRINCE

Is there any little girl or boy here who would like to sit still in a chair a-l-l day long and never go roller skating nor slide downhill on a brand-new sled? Just have nothing to do but "sit around." I do not believe you would like even to be a prince if all you could do with your beautiful toys was only to sit and look at them.

But once there was a little boy, a prince, who was not able to play with children. If he went anywhere he had to be carried. The little fellow was lame. Both his feet were crippled. The poor little prince had no mother to love him and take care of him. It would have been so much better for him if his mother had lived. We all of us know how good it is to have a mother, especially if we are unhappy and want a great deal of petting.

The little lame prince's name was Me-phi-bo-sheth. A long name for small mouths to speak. But if you take just one syllable at a time and say it slowly you will get it. Don't give up if you miss it the first time.

When the prince was a little boy only five years old there was a terrible war. His father and his grandfather were in the war. His grandfather, King Saul, and his father, Jonathan, had to leave their home and fight in a dreadful battle. So one morning they must have said good-by to the little prince, and told him what all grandfathers and fathers tell their little boys: "Be a good boy until we come back." But they never came back. His father and his grandfather, King Saul, were killed in that terrible battle.

The little prince had a good nurse who was kind to him and took care of him. She was in the king's palace alone with the little boy when she heard that all his uncles and cousins, his father, and his grandfather had been killed in the war. Now there was no one left to love him but his nurse. She was afraid to stay any longer in the king's house. The Philistines who had killed Saul and Jonathan were on their way to the palace.

Of course they would take the little prince captive and perhaps kill him, and burn down the palace. But the nurse was not going to let the Philistines get the little fellow.

She decided to run away to some of her friends and take him with her. She picked him up, threw him across her shoulder, and ran out of the palace and down the hill.

She had a long way to go, up and down steep hills and across a river. It may have been night when she ran away and so dark that she could not see where she was going. She ought to have gone slowly in the dark, but she was in such a hurry that she ran. A boy five years old is heavy, so I do not think she carried the little prince all the way. She must have put him down and told him he would have to do some running for himself. How those little feet did fly! He and his nurse were in such a hurry that the little fellow had a bad fall and hurt both his feet. The night of that terrible journey was the last time those little feet ever ran or walked. Mephibosheth was a cripple all the rest of his life.

When the little lame prince grew to be a man he found a kind friend. This friend had loved his father, Jonathan. Who do you think this good friend was? It was King

David—the one, you remember, who killed the giant Goliath. Ever since Mephibosheth and his nurse had run away from his grandfather Saul's palace King David had been fighting the troublesome Philistines. At last David drove them all out of the country. Everybody was happy and comfortable once more.

King David, you remember, loved Jonathan, the father of the little lame prince. David had promised that he would always take care of Jonathan's children. But only one little child was left and that was Mephibosheth. When King David found him he was no longer a little prince. He was a man, a big prince. Even though Mephibosheth was no longer a little boy, he needed a kind friend like King David, for he was a cripple. In those days people were not kind to cripples. Most of the time they were treated very cruelly. Sometimes cripples were made to stay out doors no matter how cold it was. Often they did not have enough to eat, and they had to beg for the little they had.

David sent for Mephibosheth to come and live with him. He was always to live in the king's palace. He was to be treated as a prince, always wear warm and beautiful clothes, and always have enough to eat every single day. Just think of it! Sit with the king at his table and be waited on as though he were King David's son! No one ever would treat Mephibosheth cruelly again, because David was his friend.

THE EWE LAMB

Once upon a time there was a very rich man. He lived in a large house on top of a high hill. His house was beautiful. Rich rugs covered the floors. The lamps were all of gold and silver. In some of the rooms there were cool, splashing fountains, but not a chair nor a table anywhere. In those days when people grew tired they sat on the floor with their feet curled under them. When they ate they sat on the floor in the same way. But it wasn't hard for them, as they had soft rugs under them and piles of comfortable cushions at their backs.

After you had gone all over this rich man's house you would want to see what he owned outside of it. There was a beautiful garden with a wealth of flowers in it, pink and blue, red and yellow, every kind of gay-colored, pretty posy. Birds sang in it, and no doubt fishes darted back and forth in the marble fountains. On the green hillsides were herds of fat cattle and flocks of woolly sheep nibbling their dinner from the grassy ground. Camels with bells about their necks the man had in plenty. Sleek oxen there were to plough his fields, and asses upon which he rode. Besides all these he had great orchards of olive trees and figs, and heavy clusters of grapes peeped out from among the vines in his vineyard.

Close by this man there lived another one who was very poor. He and his children lived in a small house with only one room in it — a mud hut, probably, or perhaps a large cave in one of the huge rocks on the hillside. The only beds these poor people had were rough, shaggy goat skins. The father had no money to buy clothes for his children, and they had no mother to make them clothes. But in that hot country poor little children went naked when they played in the burning sun. So these little folks were happy.

Sometimes when the rich man walked upon the roof in the evening he could hear the shouts of the children at play. They sang and danced outside their miserable hut, and drank their supper of goat's milk from coarse wooden bowls. The little folks had a playfellow, a little lamb that kicked up its heels and shook its woolly tail as it capered about with the children. Sometimes it put its small nose in the children's bowls and drank greedily of the milk. The little lamb slept with them at night. It was such a pretty lamb, its fleece must have been always snowy white, for the children loved their pet and wanted its soft wool

to look pure and clean. No cattle, no goats, no camels did the poor man have. Nothing but this little lamb with which his children played belonged to him. He had two hands with which he worked to earn money to buy his little ones food.

One evening the rich man saw the frisky little lamb playing with his neighbor's children. "Just the thing," said the rich man. "I have a guest tonight and I must give him a feast. That lamb will make a fine roast for my guest." Why didn't he take a sheep from his own flocks? Great juicy grapes, luscious figs, and rich olives he could have spread before his guest. But he wanted his neighbor's pet lamb, the only thing his neighbor and his children had to make them happy. What a cruel thing to do! Imagine the little children going crying to bed while the rich man and his guest were eating their pet lamb for supper!

* * * * * *

Nathan, the prophet, came and told David all about it. David was very angry. "How can anyone be so selfish and wicked?" he said. "A person without pity for the poor man deserves to die," he told Nathan. "Make that rich man give his poor neighbor many lambs in place of the one he stole away," commanded David.

The king looked fine and grand as he spoke. Every one who heard him must have said. "Isn't that just like our noble David?" Nathan did not smile; he looked sad and stern as pointing his finger at David he said, "You are the man. It is you who have done this wicked deed." Poor, poor David! Can't you see him hang his head, ashamed to look in Nathan's face? Yes, he remembered, he had taken from a poor man his only treasure. It was not a lamb he had stolen, but it was something the poor man valued, and it was all the poor man had.

Now David knew why Nathan had told him this dreadful tale of cruel greed. He, the king, had done wrong. As the king, David had a right to take away anything that he wanted from any one of his people. It was not the king's laws but God's laws that he had disobeyed. And it was God's laws that David really wished to keep, for he loved the God who had made him king. "Will God forgive my doing the very thing I am punishing other people for doing?" he must have said. What do you suppose the king did when he was alone? Fell on his face in his bedchamber, clothed himself in sackcloth, and put ashes on his head. I know he must have done so, for David was sorry and ashamed. And in David's country that is what people did when they felt sorry.

"God has blest you with peace, but since you have done this thing 'the sword shall never depart from thy house,'" Nathan told David. And it was so. Joab, the general of his army, disobeyed him, his sons quarreled, and savage neighbors kept always troubling him. He could not give back what he had taken from the poor man, for the man was dead. God had made him king and he had not been as good a king as he himself wanted to be. It was God he had forgotten when he did this wicked thing; that is why David said:

"Against Thee, Thee only
    have I sinned.
And done that which is evil
    in Thy sight."

THE RICH MAN SAW HIS NEIGHBOR'S LAMB

ABSALOM'S HAIR

How many little boys like to wear beautiful long curls? Not many, I'm sure. But there was a time when big men let their hair grow long. Some wore it curled, and oiled until it shone, or had it braided with gold thread. Absalom, King David's son, had beautiful black hair; it was long and heavy. He was proud of his hair and of his face, too, for he was praised for his beauty. The people called him the handsomest man in all Israel. He was a wicked son. He envied his father and his brothers, and wanted his father to die so that he could be king. He kept telling the people how much more he would do for them if he were chosen king, and at last the foolish people believed him.

Then Absalom and David's people banded together to turn the king out of his palace and make him leave Jerusalem. From the beautiful city poor unhappy David had to run away and hide from Absalom and his soldiers.

All the people who loved David followed him. Not one of his old soldiers or his generals deserted him. It was a long, long caravan of miserable and unhappy people that went out of the gates of Jerusalem and toiled up the slopes of Mount Olivet. They wept and wailed as they went. Was the great Kingdom of Israel going to be destroyed by a wicked usurper? Stealing a kingdom from the rightful king or trying to take his place is usurping. Absalom was trying to take the place of his own father, King David.

But Joab, the captain of David's army, did not weep; he did not even look sorry. The others might walk barefooted over the sharp stones, hold their heads down, and cover them with their mantles because they were so grieved. Joab, the warrior, had no time to cry. Absalom was a traitor and he intended not to cry over but to punish him.

"Do you know that Ahithophel, the wise man, has deserted you and is advising Absalom?" one of David's soldiers asked him.

The king answered only by saying: "O God, make the advice of Ahithophel seem foolish to Absalom!" But Hushai, David's friend, was far wiser than Ahithophel. Every one supposed Ahithophel was the wisest man in all Israel. No one ever thought of contradicting him. Hushai was wiser because he knew how to manage Absalom, and that was the one thing Ahithophel did not know.

At the top of the hill the sad caravan stopped. The people were hungry and tired. Ziba, a servant of the house of Saul, was waiting for them there. He had a fine lunch ready for them. Two asses with great packs filled full of good things to eat must have made them glad. Perhaps you would like to know what those packs on the asses' backs held: bread—loaves and loaves of it—raisins, summer fruits, and a bottle of wine. Hushai was there, too, but he did not stay. He was on his way to Jerusalem to defeat Ahithophel's counsel. No doubt he ran all the way. The first thing he did when he came to the palace was to greet Absalom with a shout and say: "Long live the king, long live the king!" These words flattered Absalom wonderfully. Can't you see him swell with royal pride when he hears himself called king? Ahithophel had never said such fine

things to him, he had only given him excellent advice. Hushai knew that the king's son liked flattery better than he liked advice, even though that advice was good. Of course Absalom listened to what Hushai told him to do, which was the worst thing he could have done. For Hushai advised him to do the very thing that would destroy him.

All through the night soldiers kept coming to David's camp and offering to fight on his side. When morning came King David had a large army ready for battle. During the night he and his soldiers had slipped down into the valley and crossed the river. Another good friend was waiting there for the

king and his soldiers. Shobi had brought beds for the men to sleep on and dishes from which they ate. That night their supper was almost a banquet. Shobi had brought barley, wheat, and parched grain, beans and lentils, honey, and butter and cheese. He even gave them sheep, for hungry soldiers like meat.

The next morning you would have seen Absalom riding on his mule with his long hair floating in the breeze. He went into the woods where the battle was fought. Much surprised he must have been to find the woods full of King David's powerful soldiers. Absalom's army was beaten. Perhaps Absalom was frightened and lost his way, or his hair may have blown in his eyes and blinded him. He surely could not have seen where he was going, for he let the mule run under a tree. Its branches were so low that they caught in his hair and pulled

him from his mule. The animal trotted on and left him hanging there. How Absalom must have struggled and thrown his arms about trying to get himself free! But his beautiful hair was long and strong and he could not tear it from the branches.

Joab saw him struggling, but he did not pity him. Absalom was a traitor and must die, the warrior thought. He killed the prince as he hung by his hair. David had commanded his generals not to harm Absalom. Joab did not obey. He was only a warrior, not Absalom's own father—that made a difference. Back into Jerusalem went the king, his people, and his soldiers. The kingdom was again David's, but David had lost his son. Up in the chamber over the gate of the city he mourned, saying, "O my son Absalom!... would I had died for thee, O Absalom, my son, my son!"

A STORY OF SOLOMON

SOLOMON'S WISDOM

It was a very, very little baby and it was to be cut in two. Dreadful, wasn't it? There are a great many things that can be divided and it doesn't hurt them a bit. But a baby!—who ever heard of a baby that was good for anything after it was cut in half like an apple? But the baby in this story must be divided. Solomon, the wise king of Israel, had said that it should be done. In the days when this baby lived no one ever thought of disobeying the king, unless he was the king's general; then sometimes he disobeyed. But ordinary people had to obey or lose their heads. No one wishes to lose his head even though it may be a poor one with nothing in it.

You may think Solomon was a wicked man or else that he disliked babies. Possibly you wonder if the baby cried so much that Solomon ordered it cut in two in order to stop its noise. You will never guess the reason if you sit up all night to think about it. I shall have to tell it to you.

King Solomon was wise. People thought he knew everything, and

great golden throne in his judgment hall while they told him all their troubles. Some of the people were quiet, others were so noisy that you could not hear the screaming of the peacocks in the king's garden. Some were crying, others were fighting as they walked. A few of them came slinking along as though they were ashamed, while a number ran so fast I'm sure by the time they reached Solomon's palace they would not have breath enough left to tell their wrongs.

The doors of the judgment hall swung open as the people crowded into the hall where Solomon sat. Then a young baby began to cry. I do not wonder, for it must have been uncomfortable. Two women were quarreling over it. I wonder they did not drop it as they fought and struggled. First one would snatch it and then the other. The women rudely pushed themselves inside the hall and came before the king. How grand he looked seated in his wonderful chair of ivory and gold! It had arms for him to lean upon and a rich, heavy canopy hung over it. People had to go up six steps to reach the king, and as they went they walked between six pairs of glistening, golden lions.

Up the steps to the throne the

he did come very near it. He knew so much that people came to him from all over the country to ask his advice. Whenever there was a quarrel he was expected to settle it.

It was early in the morning. Dewdrops were still hanging on the thirsty grass blades when a long line of people climbed the hill to the king's palace. In that country people did their traveling either very early or very late in the day. The burning sun made every one want to lie still and sleep in the middle of the day. The people were toiling slowly up the steep slopes because this was the day King Solomon was going to sit on his women ran. Both were very angry and one of them had been crying.

"What is the matter?" Solomon asked. The woman with the crying baby came close to the king. "This baby in my arms is my little son," she answered. "That other woman's baby is dead and she is trying to steal mine."

"My son is not dead, he is alive!" screamed the second woman. "She stole my baby when I was asleep and put her dead child in my arms." "The live baby is mine and the dead one is hers!" both shrieked. Both claimed the poor baby who was alive, each woman said she was his mother, and both of them nearly tore the little creature in two as they snatched him back and forth from each other's arms.

"You shall each have him," said Solomon. "I will have him divided and you shall each have half." Then he called for his sword. How its sharp edge glistened as a sunbeam shot along its blade!

The poor woman who had been crying so bitterly flung herself down before the king with outstretched arms. "Don't hurt him, oh, don't hurt him! Let the other woman have him!" she cried.

"Divide him, divide him," said the other woman. "We will neither one of us have him."

"Put up the sword," said Solomon to his soldier. "Give the baby to the woman who would not have him killed; she is his mother." Do you think the king was right? Every one in the judgment hall seemed to think so. The two women went down the steps and out into the king's beautiful garden. Two little doves upon the roof of the palace were cooing peacefully. The mother unwrapped the small bundle and held the sleeping baby close to her face. She too gave a soft coo. The baby was not crying now for it was safe in its own mother's arms.

STORIES OF ELIJAH AND ELISHA

THE CRUSE OF OIL

Isn't it fun to go barefoot? Bare feet can run faster than feet in stiff, heavy shoes. Listen to a story about a man who never wore shoes. His name was Elijah. He was tall and straight and a fleet runner. He ran so fast that even the king's horses couldn't keep up with him.

People who didn't like Elijah called him the "hairy man." His long unkempt black hair hung over his shoulders. Sometimes it fell over his face and into his eyes. I don't think the sun or the wind ever had a chance to burn his face, for it was covered with a bushy beard and thick whiskers.

He wore the queerest clothes. You and I would not call them clothes. When Elijah was cold he threw a woolly sheepskin around his shoulders. He always wore a skirt—a ragged sheepskin that only came to his knees. Of course, he had a leather belt, and a big pocket in his sheepskin cape.

Elijah wanted to go to a city by the seashore where he could get some water. No clouds filled with refreshing rain came to Elijah's country. The hot sun, like a great ball of fire, was burning up all the beautiful green things. The little brooks had stopped dancing over the pebbles. All the water in them had run away from the burning sun and hidden itself underneath the big stones. The grass had lost its beautiful green color and looked scorched and yellow. Poor hungry lambs and bony cattle nibbled away at the bare ground. "Water, water, water!" everything and everybody were calling. But not a raindrop answered them.

There were many dolls in that country. You would have called them dolls, for they looked just like dolls. Only they were very ugly and made of wood and stone. Some were so large that a girl or a boy could have stood inside of them. Others were so tiny that people hung them on chains which they wore around their necks. Everybody, big and little, had a doll. But they did not have the dolls to play with. The foolish people called these dolls, idols. And what do you think they did with them? They prayed to them as though they were gods.

The wicked king and queen of this country had taught the people to pray to these wooden-doll idols. Elijah would not pray to them. His God was the real God who loved His people and wanted to help them. While the people starved the heartless king and queen sometimes spread a fine dinner before their idol. Think of trying to feed a stick of wood that could not even open its mouth, while sick babies and dear little children were dying

because they could not get enough to eat! Elijah had told the king, who was a very bad king, that rain would never again fall in his country until he stopped praying to these doll idols, for Elijah knew it was God who sends us rain and gives us food.

God told Elijah to go to a city by the seashore where he would find water and food. There was a poor widow living in that city who would help Elijah. When he came to the city gates there was no one in sight but one poor woman. She looked pale and sick as if she were starving. "This must be the woman God has told to help me," thought Elijah.

"Will you bring me some water and some bread?" he asked her. The woman stopped picking up kindling sticks and started to get

him some water. But she turned back again, saying, "I have only enough barley meal and oil to make a cake for my little son and myself. As soon as that is gone we shall die, for we can never get anything more to eat."

And what do you think Elijah told her? *"Do not be afraid.* Make me a cake first, for God will keep your jar full of barley meal and your cruse full of oil 'until the day that Jehovah sendeth rain upon the earth.'"

She went back into her house and scooped out the last bit of barley meal from her jar and shook the last drop of oil from the cruse. How closely her hungry little boy must have watched her as she made the cake! After it was baked she carried it to Elijah. Then back she ran to her empty jar and there it stood full of barley meal. She took up her cruse and showed her little boy that it was full of the best oil. Now they could each have more than one cake for their supper. They would have all they needed to eat. Elijah, the widow, and her little boy never were hungry any more, for "the jar of meal wasted not, neither did the cruse of oil fail, according to the word of Jehovah, which He spake by Elijah."

THE LITTLE SICK BOY

What fun it is to play on the seashore with your shovel and pail! There you can make all shapes of sand pies and cakes. Just as they are ready for baking, swish! swash! in comes a hungry wave and carries all your sand cookies away. But it is easy to make your cakes again and fun to feed the greedy sea.

Once a little boy lived with his mother near the seashore. Every day he splashed in the water and dug his bare toes into the sand. He had no playmates, not even a brother or sister. To keep from being lonely he made friends with the sea birds. He often called to the great stormy petrel and asked for a ride on his back. The screams of the sea gulls as they rocked on the waves made him wish to be a bird in a water cradle. But he was only a little boy. All he could do was to answer the cries of the gulls with a shout while he clapped his hands and rolled over on the sand. One very solemn bird, a pelican, stood alone on a rocky ledge, with one foot drawn up under its feathers and its great bill held close to its breast. The little boy must often have been lonely and no doubt tried to make friends with the pelican.

But he was very happy with his

THE LITTLE BOY MADE FRIENDS WITH THE SEA BIRDS

feathered friends. He had always been happy in his home with his mother. But several times when he had come home with his robe full of small, curious shells and had asked his mother to look at them she had pushed him away. Her eyes were red and he knew that she had been crying. One night he and his mother went to bed without any supper. When morning came she had only a single barley cake to give him and she herself ate nothing.

Large black circles settled under his mother's eyes. The boy's little, loose shirt, which once had fitted

his plump shoulders now slipped from the small bones. Perhaps it was easier for him to wear nothing at all, like many small boys in his country. There were many whole days when neither of them had anything to eat. Perhaps they stayed in their beds and slept as hungry people often do where food is scarce.

Then a kind old man came to live with them. His name was Elijah. While this good friend stayed with them the little boy and his mother had plenty to eat. You remember the hungry boy who watched while his mother poured the last drop of oil out of her cruse and took the last handful of meal out of her jar to make a cake for Elijah? This was the little boy who had no playmates but the birds. He must have been a generous little fellow. Though he was so hungry, I'm sure he shared his thin cake of bread with the small sparrows that built their nests under his window.

It was a hungry time for everybody. The boy's cheeks grew pale and hollow, and his hands were so thin they looked like birds' claws. Of course he and his mother were never hungry after Elijah came to live with them, but the little fellow had already grown so weak that even plenty to eat did not help him. He did not go out on the seashore any more to play with the birds. When a saucy sparrow hopped into his window and flew away with a piece of his cake he did not even laugh. One morning when his mother called him he did not answer. He heard her, but his voice seemed so far away he could not use it. His mother called again. Then she came to him and said, "My precious boy, why are you so sick?" He put his cold little hand over hers, closed his eyes — and lay perfectly still.

Did his mother stop to cry? No, she knew that Elijah could help her, and he did. He took the little boy out of his mother's arms and carried him to his own room. Elijah knew that if he could only get the little boy warm again he would get well. So when he laid him on the bed Elijah did a strange thing. He stretched himself over the child to get him warm. "O Jehovah, my God, I pray thee, let this child's soul come into him again," Elijah asked of God, as he bent over the silent little figure on the bed. And Jehovah, Elijah's God, heard. Of course, He answered. The cold little body grew warm. The tired eyes must have opened with a sparkle in them. The once feeble, childish voice no doubt shouted gleefully as Elijah carried the well and happy boy down to his mother. How joyfully she must

have hugged and kissed him! She may have been so glad that she never even saw the hungry sparrows fluttering their wings over some pieces of bread they had stolen.

What do you suppose she said to Elijah? "Now I know that thou art a man of God, and that the word of Jehovah in thy mouth is truth," she told him. She and her boy were happy once more. Even when Elijah left them a few days afterward I think that she must have sung to herself as she listened to her little son calling happily to the gulls on the seashore.

117

ELIJAH'S
WONDERFUL MANTLE

Let us pretend that we are out taking a walk. It is such great fun to pretend. The grown-ups do not begin to know what good times we can have if we "just pretend." Suppose we pretend we are walking with Elijah, the "hairy man," and his friend Elisha. We will take a long, long walk with them.

We will wear our shoes, button up our coats, and have on our hats. How funny we shall look to everybody we meet! Remember, we are pretending that we are in a strange country, and a long, long way from home. A country where the women go about with their faces tied up

in long white bags. They call them veils, but to you and me those white things look like bags. The long bag-veils cover all the face except the eyes. How would you like to wear one? In this country the men wear such queer clothes. Elijah has no shoes. He never in his life has had on a pair. He wears a short sheepskin skirt that doesn't always cover his knees. A coarse, woolly sheepskin is thrown around his shoulders for a mantle. But Elijah doesn't need anything better to wear for he spends most of his time on the hot sands of the desert. When night comes he creeps under some bushes and goes to sleep. Sometimes when he is on the mountains he crawls into a cave for a night's rest. He doesn't like cities. He will not live in them. He only visits them when he goes to tell people they will be punished for being so wicked.

Elisha is going on this long walk too. When you look at him you will think he is dressed for a party instead of a tramp in the mountains. His clothes are quite different from Elijah's. They are not short and ragged but are white and long; a fine long overcloak reaches to his feet and almost covers them. His hair does not fall over his face and tumble down his back in stringy locks as Elijah's does. Elisha's hair is short and neatly brushed. He does not like to get his feet torn on the sharp stones nor soiled by desert sands. So he always wears handsome sandals with embroidered straps. Elisha never could beat the king's horses in a race as Elijah did. Elisha prefers to walk, so he carries a staff to lean on when he wants to rest.

Which one do you want to travel with, Elijah or Elisha? I can guess. It is Elisha. Elijah, the "hairy man," always makes us feel as though we had been naughty. But Elisha smiles so sweetly that we know he sees that we are sorry and are going to be better. Elisha doesn't like dark, smelly caves nor lonely deserts. He lives in the city in a house where he can shut the doors and windows and keep out the cold. How many little girls and boys think they would like to live in a cave? It might be fun in the daytime, but when night came how we would wish we were at home in our beds close to mother!

Now let us pretend that we have started on our walk. Where do you suppose Elijah and Elisha are going? I think they are climbing down a steep mountain side. The path is dreadfully rough and the loose stones make them slip and slide as they journey down. A little brook is singing as it rushes down the mountain side, "Come thirsty people, come drink my cool fresh water." But Elijah and Elisha do not stop.

Elijah always seems to be in a hurry. He is today. But fast as he travels Elisha is keeping up with him. "Jehovah has sent for me," Elijah says to Elisha. "Do not follow me, stay here."

And Elisha replies, "I shall not leave you."

Soon they come to a city named Bethel. Perhaps they will stop here

and rest a bit. In this city there are some good people who always pray to the God of Elijah and Elisha. These good people come out to meet Elijah and Elisha. Elisha, who likes cities and enjoys company, stops and talks with them. These people tell Elisha that he will come back from his walk but Elijah never will, because he is going away forever.

Elijah tells Elisha he should stay in Bethel with his friends. Elisha will not do it. Wherever Elijah goes he is determined to follow. They pass another big city and

more people meet them and tell Elisha that Elijah is going away forever. But Elisha knew it all the time. Once more Elijah advises Elisha not to go any farther with him. "Jehovah has sent me to the Jordan," Elijah says.

"I shall never leave you," answers Elisha.

Down the rough mountain side, across scorched plains, and on past beautiful cities we have hurried to see where Elijah is going. Will he never stop? This is what you and I are thinking as we pretend we are walking with him. Yes, by the River Jordan he stops for a minute and takes off his rough mantle. Then he rolls it up in a tight bundle and strikes the river with it. We are wondering if he is angry because the river has stopped him. Let us pretend we are watching and see what happens. Oh, isn't it wonderful! Where the mantle touches the water a path is made through it. The river divides and a strip of dry sand runs from one bank to the other. It makes a path just wide enough for Elijah and Elisha to cross over without getting wet.

But why does Elisha cross the river? He has no mantle. How can he get back again to the other side? "What shall I give you before I leave you?" Elijah asks Elisha.

I think I know what Elisha wants. Do you? He wants that wonderful mantle of Elijah's. So he asks Elijah for it. With that wonderful mantle Elisha thinks he can make every one happy. Elijah's mantle will make any one who wears it wish to do good. It will show him how to do all he wishes to do. Elisha loves people. He wants to see the sick healed, and every one who is sad he wants to make happy. He is sure that if he has Elijah's wonderful mantle he can do all these good things.

"If you see me when I leave, you may have it," Elijah told him. Now we know why Elisha kept so close to Elijah. He is going to be near Elijah when he is carried away, so near that he can see him. While they were talking Elisha thinks he sees a chariot with horses. The chariot drives right between the prophet and Elisha. In all his life Elisha has never seen a chariot like this one. The horses and chariot are of fire. For just a moment he sees them. Then they are gone. A dreadful hurricane begins to blow. It tosses Elisha's long white robe over his head. When he pushes it back the wind is carrying Elijah away. Elisha is alone. He is right where Elijah was when he last saw him. Elisha's eyes have seen, and at his feet is Elijah's wonderful mantle.

POISONED POTTAGE

What do people do when they are hungry? "Eat, of course," every one answers. But suppose there is nothing to eat? Then little cheeks grow hollow and small fingers look as though the bones might push through the skin. In some countries little children always are hungry. There is not enough food to give every one something to eat. Elisha lived in just such a country. People ploughed the ground with their oxen and sowed their seed. Then out from the earth shot tiny green blades, every one of them looking straight up to the sun and the clouds. As they waved back and

forth in the wind they must have nodded to one another and called to the clouds to give them water and to the sun to give them light. In Elisha's country the sun was not always friendly, it sometimes burned up every green thing with its fierce, hot rays. The wind helped the sun to be disagreeable, for it often drove the clouds away, so far away that not a thirsty animal or plant had a drop of water to drink.

When these dry seasons came the people went hungry. When there was no water, nothing grew, and that meant nothing to eat. Elisha, who was always helping people, took his staff, slipped on his long white robe, belted it in tight so that

he could walk fast, and started for Gilgal. It was a poor time to make a visit there, for the people of Gilgal were having a famine. That means there was nothing to eat. If the folks in Gilgal did not have enough food for themselves surely there was not enough for Elisha. But the prophet did not expect the people to make a feast for him. He knew they were hungry and he intended to show them how they could have a good dinner. Elisha was not going *for* something, he was going to *give* something. I once knew a dear little boy who must have been like Elisha. As he started off to a party his mother asked him, "Why do you go to the party, Johnny?" and he answered, "To make some one happy, Mother."

"Set the biggest kettle over the fire and boil some pottage," were the first words Elisha spoke to his servant when he reached Gilgal. There were plenty of pots and pans and probably there was a fine fire, but there was nothing but water to boil — not much of a dinner for hungry people. "Go into the field and gather some vegetables for the pottage," Elisha told the men who were sitting around him. Off several of them started. To have a vegetable stew for their dinner was enough to make all hungry men run to find something for it. There was not much to find, for the sun had dried up nearly everything. One wild vine had some queer-looking round things growing on it. They were really gourds and there were lots of them, plenty for the biggest kind of a stew. A man filled his bosom full, and started back with his load. The people were very hungry but they did not like the looks of those green gourds in the man's bosom. Nobody knew what they were and all the men were afraid of them.

Into the pot went the gourds and soon was ready a nice thick pottage for the men. "Pour it out," said Elisha. They all pushed eager pairs of hands into the bowl of pottage and then thrust some of it into their

mouths. But oh, what wry faces! After the first mouthful each man spat it upon the ground. It must have been bitter. In those hot countries people like everything to be sweet. They will drink dirty water because it is sweet, and not touch clear, sparkling water that has no taste.

"There is death in the pot!" they cried to Elisha. The prophet did not call them foolish and say they must eat the pottage or go hungry. I told you that Elisha was kind. He felt sorry for the people when they were afraid the pottage was poisoned, so he said, "Bring some meal and put it in the pot." The meal must have taken away the strange, bitter taste. When the bad taste was gone they were willing to eat the pottage. After the meal went into the vegetable stew the men ate it with relish. There was no harm in the pot for them.

Elisha seldom scolded or found fault with people and of course they all loved him. He had such a sweet voice that it made people who heard him speak want to be better. All their ugly feelings seemed to fly away before the kindly words of Elisha. His whole heart was full of love for everything and everybody. Only one other in the Bible loved as did Elisha. How many of you little folks can tell who that is?

ELISHA'S GUESTS

Israel's bad neighbors were again troubling her. Little bands of rough Syrian soldiers stole into the mountains and hid themselves so that they might spring upon the king of Israel and make him and his soldiers captives. Elisha knew what these wicked neighbors were trying to do and he warned Israel's king.

"The king of Israel is never where I expect to find him," complained the king of Syria. "Some of my own soldiers surely must be traitors."

"Not so," answered a Syrian, "it is Elisha. He knows the words you speak secretly in your own room, and because he knows, he tells the king of Israel what you intend to do and where you intend to go."

How could the Syrians close Elisha's mouth? By making him a prisoner, of course. And that is what the Syrian king tried to do. "Go to the city of Dothan, where Elisha lives, and surround it with soldiers," commanded the king of Syria. Chariots and horses, soldiers with swords and deadly bows and arrows, crept softly along through the night to Dothan. They had no light but the stars, for no one must see them stealing upon the sleeping prophet alone in his house with his servant. They reached the city and made a circle around it. Not a move could Elisha make without meeting the point of a sharp Syrian spear.

In the early morning Elisha's servant looked out of the window. His eyes must have nearly popped out of his head when he saw that great army. Soldiers, soldiers, everywhere, and not a way to escape. "What shall we do, master, oh, what shall we do?" he called to Elisha.

"First of all, stop being afraid," his master answered. "There are many more fighting with us than are fighting with these Syrians." Elisha did not tremble. Jehovah, God, was with him and that gave the prophet more strength than all the Syrian host and its king. Then Elisha spoke quietly——he was talking to God. "Open my servant's eyes and let him see," he was saying. Before the astonished eyes of the boy there appeared a wonderful scene. The mountain was filled with horses and chariots of fire. The army of God was round about Elisha. Stronger than a ring of iron it stood between the Syrian host and the prophet.

The Syrians did not see the army that was fighting for Elisha, so on they came to capture him. Elisha said to God, "Smite this people,

I pray thee, with blindness." The Syrian soldiers staggered and stumbled about, throwing their arms around wildly to feel where they were going. Every one of the Syrians was now blind and trying to grope his way out of the valley. Elisha met them. "Follow me, and I will bring you to the man whom ye seek," he told them. What a strange procession it was, all those savage-looking soldiers led by the sweet-faced Elisha! And where do you suppose they went? Right into Samaria where the king of Israel and his army lived. In Samaria the Syrian soldiers lost their

blindness. They saw that instead of catching Elisha in a trap they themselves had been caught.

You may be sure the king of Israel was delighted. His enemies were now in his power. He might never find them so again. Now was his opportunity to kill every one of them. Who would think of letting enemies escape? Elisha did. So when the king of Israel said, "Shall I smite them?" Elisha answered, "No." He had taught these Syrian soldiers that faith in God was power. Only spiteful people wish to injure others. But Elisha was so full of love there was not a corner in his heart big enough to hold a hateful thought.

Did he let the Syrians go? You know he did. But before they went on that long journey home Elisha gave them a splendid dinner. It was really a feast. There must have been figs and dates, perhaps a roasted lamb or calf, great bunches of raisins and big purple grapes, bread, and delicious camels' milk. Do you feel like making a wry face? Do not do so, for where Elisha lived camels' milk was considered a fine drink.

If the Syrians had been guests instead of robbers Elisha could not have treated them better. Soon every man had eaten enough and Elisha sent them home. Do you suppose they were grateful? They must have been, for the Syrians never troubled Israel again during Elisha's lifetime.